"Mr. Adams," Mayor Russell said, "your coming along may end up being very fortunate for us."

"In what way, Mayor?"

"Well," he said, "there are factions here and in town who want to leave here. We've been able to dissuade them up to now, but they are growing in number. It's the sheriff's job to keep them from leaving town, and our deputy's job is to keep them from leaving here, but . . ."

"Say no more, Mayor," Clint said. "I'd be glad to lend a hand."

DON'T MISS THESE
ALL-ACTION WESTERN SERIES
FROM THE BERKLEY PUBLISHING GROUP

THE GUNSMITH by J. R. Roberts

Clint Adams was a legend among lawmen, outlaws, and ladies. They called him . . . the Gunsmith.

LONGARM by Tabor Evans

The popular long-running series about U.S. Deputy Marshal Long—his life, his loves, his fight for justice.

SLOCUM by Jake Logan

Today's longest-running action Western. John Slocum rides a deadly trail of hot blood and cold steel.

BUSHWHACKERS by B. J. Lanagan

An action-packed series by the creators of Longarm! The rousing adventures of the most brutal gang of cutthroats ever assembled—Quantrill's Raiders.

DIAMONDBACK by Guy Brewer

Dex Yancey is Diamondback, a southern gentleman turned con man when his brother cheats him out of the family fortune. Ladies love him. Gamblers hate him. But nobody pulls one over on Dex . . .

WILDGUN by Jack Hanson

Will Barlow's continuing search for his daughter, kidnapped by the Blackfeet Indians who slaughtered the rest of his family.

THE GUNSMITH

227

SAFETOWN

J. R. ROBERTS

JOVE BOOKS, NEW YORK

This is a work of fiction. Names, characters, places, and incidents are either the product of the author's imagination or are used fictitiously, and any resemblance to actual persons, living or dead, business establishments, events, or locales is entirely coincidental.

SAFETOWN

A Jove Book / published by arrangement with
the author

PRINTING HISTORY
Jove edition / November 2000

The Penguin Putnam Inc. World Wide Web site address is
http://www.penguinputnam.com

ISBN: 0-515-12958-5

A JOVE BOOK®
Jove Books are published by The Berkley Publishing Group,
a division of Penguin Putnam Inc.,
375 Hudson Street, New York, New York 10014.
JOVE and the "J" design
are trademarks belonging to Penguin Putnam Inc.

PRINTED IN THE UNITED STATES OF AMERICA

10 9 8 7 6 5 4 3 2 1

ONE

Clint Adams heard the flies before he saw them. It was an ominous buzzing that caused him to rein Eclipse in for a moment before continuing. When he finally came upon the scene he reined his horse in again, this time in horror. The smell gagged him and caused Eclipse to become agitated. He turned the horse and walked him a distance away before dismounting and tying his lead to a bush. He then walked back to survey the scene again.

Someone had used a dried-up creek bed as a mass grave, and great big blue and green flies were buzzing about, feeding on the corpses. The bodies had been dumped in on top of one another. Clint tried to count the bodies but kept losing count at a dozen, as he was unable to discern which bodies certain arms and legs belonged to. He was dismayed, though, to see that there were at least two women in the jumble of limbs.

It was midday and the sun was high. Some of the bodies obviously had been dead longer than others and had been exposed to the sun longer. Indeed, some of them seemed to have exploded as gas had built up inside

1

of them. A couple of the bodies were completely covered by the flies, others were not yet being fed upon as they had not been there long enough to begin their decay.

In fact, one of the bodies seemed to still be alive.

The smell of decayed and putrid flesh was like something solid in the air. Clint changed his position, seeking to use the wind to deflect the smell. When he'd found a vantage point from where he could stand he once again peered down at the body that seemed to still be moving. Finally, he decided he had to go down and take a look. As he took a step down great gouts of flies flew up into the air, almost striking him in the face. They were buzzing loudly, angry at having their meal interrupted. He was about to take another step when a voice said, "Stop . . . don't . . ."

He realized that the voice had come from the body that was still breathing.

"Are you . . . all right?" It sounded like a stupid question even as it flew from Clint's mouth.

"No," the man said. "Don't come down here. Get . . . away."

"But . . . you don't belong down there."

"I will . . . soon," the man said. "I have the . . . sickness . . ."

"The what?"

"Don't come closer," the man said. "Get away or you'll get it."

"You mean, all these people died of a . . . a sickness?"

"Yes," the man said. "Get away!" His tone became urgent.

"But . . . you can't stay there."

"I'm going to die soon," the man said. "They knew

that . . . when they dropped me in here. I—I don't blame
'em . . ."

"Mister," Clint said, "I've got to help you—"

"You can help me," the man said.

"How?"

"Kill me," the man said. "End my suffering."

"I can't kill you in cold blood."

"Mister," the man said, "I'm done for. I got the fever,
the sores . . . I can't see . . . I'm blind . . . you gotta help
me. Please. Kill me."

"W-what town are you from?"

"Thanesville," the man said. "But don't go there. Go
to . . . Safetown."

"Safetown?"

"West of town," the man said. "It's . . . safe there. Nobody's sick."

"All right," Clint said, "I'll go to Safetown. I can take
you there—"

"Mister, please!" the man cried, a sob tearing his
voice. "There's critters out here . . . don't let them eat
me alive. Please, put me out of my misery. The least
you can do is send me to meet my maker . . . with some
dignity."

The irony of a man lying amid a mass of rancid dead
bodies, talking about dying with dignity, did not escape
Clint and did, indeed, touch him.

"Mister?" the man called. "Mister, you still there?"
The panic in his voice touched Clint even deeper.

"I'm here."

"Will ya do it for me?" the man asked. "Will ya?
Huh?"

"Sure," Clint said, "sure, friend, I'll . . . I'll do it for
you."

"Just do it quick, will ya? Don't tell me when you're gonna—"

One shot from Clint's gun cut the man off in mid-sentence. He took the time to eject the spent shell and replace it with a live one before returning the weapon to his holster. He felt like he should say something over the man—maybe over all of them—but he couldn't think of anything. The shot had scattered the rest of the flies, but some of the brave ones—or the hungrier ones—were already coming back.

Clint walked around the mass grave and back to where he had left Eclipse. The animal could still smell the rotting flesh and was still agitated.

"Don't worry, boy," Clint said, soothingly, patting the big black Arabian's neck, "we're leaving."

He walked Eclipse farther away from the gruesome scene before he stopped to mount him. He thought briefly of the man he had killed. He'd taken the man at his word that he wanted to die, that he was beyond help. The only way he could live with what he did was to justify it by thinking he'd done the man a favor. No man should be left to die like that, tossed in among the dead, left to the scavengers like flies and buzzards and who knew what else, left to be eaten alive. Whoever had dropped him into that grave deserved to be horse-whipped, and Clint swore that if he found out who it was, he was going to see to it.

TWO

About a mile farther down the road Clint came to the sign that said: THANESVILLE. It was a wooden sign, and where it said POP. the number had been whited out and not replaced. Beneath that, in white paint, somebody had written the words *Quarantined. Do Not Enter.*

Apparently, what the man had said was true. Thanesville was in the grip of some disease and the bodies he had seen in that mass grave were the victims—so far.

West of town, the dying man had said, was a place called Safetown.

"Come on, Eclipse," Clint said, "let's go see if we can find it."

He turned the horse west and moved on . . .

Jenny Thane had completed what had become her morning ritual—checking all of the residents of Safetown to make sure they were not exhibiting any symptoms of the disease that was destroying Thanesville, a town her father had built. When she reached her tent, Horace Russell, the mayor of Thanesville, was waiting for her, sitting in a chair. Russell had known Jenny's father very well and considered her the daughter he'd never had. When her father died he promised that he would look out for her. As mayor, he was supposed to look out for the whole town—but look what had happened . . .

"Jenny?" he asked, as she approached.

"Nothing, Uncle Horace," she said.

"Are you sure?"

"Yes," she said, "I'm sure."

"You couldn't have missed something?"

"Doc Beacham told me exactly what to look for," Jenny said, "and I *am* a nurse, Uncle Horace."

"I know, I know," he said, taking her hand. "I'm not doubting you, dear. I just wish Doc Beacham had come here with us instead of staying . . . there."

"He had to stay in town and care for the sick and dying, Uncle," she said, "you know that. It's his responsibility."

"It's his responsibility to care for the living, not the dead," Russell said. "And it's his responsibility to make sure he doesn't get the damned disease himself."

"He had to stay," she said, again. "It was all he could do. He's that kind of man."

"I know what kind of man Ed Beacham is, Jenny," Russell said. "He's my best friend."

Jenny squeezed Russell's hand and said, "He'll be all right, Uncle. You'll see."

"You look tired, dear. Get some rest."

She was tired. She checked all the residents of Safetown before they went to bed and again when they got up in the morning. She was also called out in the middle of the night when someone thought they were exhibiting symptoms. It did not leave her much time to sleep.

"I'll try to get some sleep," she said, going into her tent. From inside she called, "Wake me if anything happens."

"I will," Russell said. "I will."

What was going to happen? he thought. A miracle? Even though all of the healthy residents of Thanesville were now safely residing in the tented community called Safetown, they all fully expected to fall victim to the disease and die, themselves. Anyone who survived this epidemic was going to be totally shocked.

Russell touched his own throat, probing for any swelling, and checked his flesh for sores. Nothing, but that didn't mean he wasn't going to get it.

He and two other members of the eight-man town council were in Safetown. The sheriff was still in town, but his deputy was here. One hundred and forty-seven people had come out here, erected tents and were now living there, waiting for the inevitable. That left over two hundred still in town, and that was not counting the ones who had already died of the disease.

He looked up as he heard approaching footsteps and saw Sam Evers, one of the other council members approaching.

"Horace," Evers said.

"Sam. Pull up a chair."

Chairs were all they had, those and some crude cots that had also been built by the carpenter, Dave Ricketts. Everything else these one hundred and forty-seven people owned had to be left in town. They were allowed to take nothing with them. The clothes and bedding they had had been donated to them—from a distance—by people from surrounding farms and ranches.

Sam Evers pulled over one of the rickety chairs and

lowered himself into it. Both he and Russell were in their sixties, had been through a lot in their lives, but had never seen the likes of this disease.

And neither had Doc Beacham.

Russell hoped that Evers would not ask him the same question he had been asking him for weeks: "What are we going to do?" He still didn't have an answer. Luckily, he was saved by the question by the sound of an approaching rider. Both men grabbed for the rifles they kept close at hand. If it was someone from town, they might have to kill him rather then allow him to infect them and the other residents of Safetown.

They held their rifles ready, and waited.

THREE

There was no sign to identify the cluster of tents as Safetown, but Clint couldn't imagine what else this could
have been. As he approached he saw two men watching
him, holding rifles nervously. They were joined by a
much younger man wearing a badge, who was also holding a rifle.

"Hold it right there!" one of the older men called to
him. "Don't come any closer."

Clint reined in, because nothing scared him more than
a nervous man with a gun.

"Is this Safetown?" he asked.

"Who wants to know?" the spokesman asked.

"My name is Clint Adams."

That stopped the conversation for a moment as the
three men exchanged a look.

"The Gunsmith?" the man with the badge asked.

"That's right."

"Did you come through town?" the first man asked.

"No," Clint said, "I came from the other direction."

A woman stepped out of a tent behind the men and stopped to listen.

"How did you know what this place is called?" the spokesman asked.

"A man told me."

"What man?"

"I didn't get his name," Clint said. "He was lying in a mass grave, covered by flies and surrounded by—"

"Alive?" the woman called out, in shock. "He was in that grave and still alive?"

"That's right."

She looked incensed.

"I don't believe it!" she said to no one in particular. She looked at Clint and, oddly, the men deferred to her suddenly. "What happened to him?"

"Well, Ma'am," Clint said, "he told me he was sick and dying and blind. He begged me to put him out of his misery."

"And did you?" she asked.

"I'm almost ashamed to say I did."

"You shot him?" the deputy asked.

"Yes."

"God bless you," the woman said.

"Thank you, Ma'am, for that thought, but I don't think the Almighty'll be doing that for me any time soon."

"Mister Adams," she said, "this is very important. Did you touch anyone in that grave?"

"No, Ma'am," he said. "The man I . . . helped, he made sure I didn't get too close."

"That's good," she said. "Gentlemen, put away your guns."

"Are we gonna take his word for that?" the third man

asked. "That he didn't touch anyone? Didn't come from town?"

"I am willing to take his word," the woman said. "I suggest you do the same, Mr. Evers."

The man called Evers exchanged a glance with the deputy, who didn't look too sure himself.

"Uncle Horace," she said to the spokesman.

"Put your guns away, gentlemen," the man said. "Mr. Adams, come ahead and we'll show you as much hospitality as we can in our current situation."

"I'm grateful, sir," Clint said, "and ma'am."

Clint gave Eclipse a little kick with his heels and rode him into their midst.

They got someone to take Eclipse from Clint to take care of him and then gave Clint a chair to sit in. He could see that the chair had recently been handmade.

"That's the best we can do, I'm afraid," the woman said.

"It's fine."

"Allow me to introduce everyone," she said. "I'm Jenny Thane, this is Horace Russell, the mayor of . . . of Thanesville, and now of Safetown. That man is Sam Evers, a member of the town council, and over here is our deputy, Jace Cole."

"Gentlemen," Clint said.

Another old woman approached and handed Clint a cup of coffee.

"Lunch is almost ready," she said to everyone and returned to her duties—presumably, as head cook.

"Mr. Adams," Jenny said, "I'm afraid you've ridden into a terrible situation. Our town has been stricken with a deadly disease."

"So the man in the, uh, grave told me."

"I wish we could figure out who that was," Jenny said, and then with more fervor, "and I wish to God I knew who put him in that grave while he was still alive!"

"I'd like to find that out myself," Clint said, sipping the coffee.

"Maybe they thought he was dead," Mayor Russell said.

"That's possible," Jenny said, "but Doc Beacham wouldn't make that kind of mistake."

"Where are your doctor and your sheriff?" Clint asked.

"Still in Thanesville," Jenny said, "along with most of our population. We are some hundred and forty-seven people who were deemed healthy enough to leave."

"Your doctor was taken ill?"

"No," Jenny said, "but he felt a responsibility to stay and tend to those who were."

"A brave man."

"Yes," Jenny said, "he is."

"And the sheriff?" Clint asked.

"He had come into direct contact with some of the sick," Jenny said. "He thought it best not to leave."

"And would that be Henry Ives?" Clint asked.

"Yes," Jenny said, "do you know Sheriff Ives?"

"I do, indeed," Clint said. "He's the reason I was coming here—or, to Thanesville. I was planing on visiting him."

"Well," Jenny said, "I just don't think that will be possible, Mr. Adams. Not now."

"When do you think it will be possible, Miss Thane."

She hesitated, then said, "Possibly never, Mr. Adams. Possibly never."

FOUR

It was decided that, over lunch, Jenny Thane would be the one to fill Clint in on what had been happening in Thanesville for almost a month. Others—like Mayor Russell and Mr. Evers—sat around and listened, but did not interrupt.

"It started with one sick boy," she said, "and quickly developed into an epidemic. It took us quite a while to break the town up into two factions, those who had been in direct contact with the ill, and those who had not. We quickly moved the uninfected out here, and I came along to care for them while the doctor stayed in town. I am, you see, a trained nurse."

"I assumed that," Clint said. "Tell me how could you be so sure that all of these people were uninfected?"

"We were as sure as we could be," she said. "I check everyone each night and each morning for symptoms."

"What about your supplies?"

"Our town carpenter is among us. He built some chairs, cots and tables, while other supplies have been

13

brought to us by nearby farmers and ranchers who were willing to help."

"Decent of them."

"They won't come too close to us, though, any more than they'll go into town. They leave the items in a clearing and then we pick them up. That goes for food, too."

"And how long do you expect this situation to last?" he asked. "I mean, the separation of Thanesville and Safetown?"

"We don't know," she said. "We can only depend on what Doc Beacham tells us."

"Is everyone susceptible?"

"No," she said, "apparently, there are some people who are immune."

"And where are they?" Clint asked. "Here or in Thanesville?"

"In town."

"Why?"

The doctor feels that while they are immune, they may actually be carriers," she said. "We can't risk letting them out of town."

"You risked bringing a hundred and forty-seven out."

"To save them," Jenny said, "but no one is permitted to leave here until . . . well, until Doc Beacham tells us."

"And the doctor?" Clint asked. "He shows no signs of symptoms?"

"Not yet," she said.

Here Mayor Russell interjected and said, "Not yet."

"Well," Clint said, "he may be one of the lucky ones who is immune. When is the last time you talked with him, or anyone from town?"

"A couple of days ago," she said. "He and I meet at

a certain point between here and town to exchange information."

"And the sheriff was still all right?"

"Yes," she said, "as of two days ago."

"Well, that's good," Clint said. "Maybe he's also one of the lucky ones who is immune."

"Mr. Adams," Mayor Russell said, "your coming along may end up being very fortunate for us."

"In what way, Mayor?"

"Well," he said, "there are factions here and in town who want to leave here. We've been able to dissuade them up to now, but they are growing in number. It's the sheriff's job to keep them from leaving town and our deputy's job to keep them from leaving here, but . . ." He stopped and looked up. The deputy had joined them, probably just moments before.

"Go ahead, Mayor," Jace Cole said. "Tell him."

"We're afraid Jace might not be able to stop them much longer," Russell said.

"I ain't ashamed of that," Deputy Cole said. "They're growin' in number, Mr. Adams. If I can't stop them and they leave they might carry this disease with them."

"He needs help," Russell said, "and I'm afraid that Sam here and myself won't be much help to him, nor will some of the others. We're merchants, you see, and—"

"Say no more, Mayor," Clint said. "I'd be glad to lend a hand, if it's all right with the deputy."

"I'd be obliged to you, Mr. Adams," Deputy Cole said.

"Good lad," Russell said. "Jace is a good lad, Mr. Adams. You can depend on him."

"And he can depend on me," Clint said. He stood and

shook hands with the young deputy, who seemed both impressed and relieved.

"I do have one favor to ask, though," Clint said.

"Name it," Russell said.

"It's of Miss Thane."

"What is it?" she asked, warily.

"When is the next time you are to go and meet with the doctor?" Clint asked.

"Tomorrow afternoon, at two."

"I'd like to go with you."

She looked at Russell, and then back at Clint.

"I don't see why not, Mr. Adams."

"And I don't see why you shouldn't start calling me Clint," he said. "All of you."

"Clint it is," Mayor Russell said.

"Now maybe I should get acquainted with Deputy Cole," Clint said. "Gentlemen—and ma'am—will you excuse me? Jace, let's go for a walk."

"Yes, sir."

FIVE

"Tell me who the trouble is coming from," Clint said to the deputy as they walked away.

"Well, there's a bunch led by a fella named Robak," Jace said. "Eight, maybe nine of them now. I been waiting for them to make another move ever since they came to be that many."

"Eight or nine at most?"

"Maybe more, by now," Jace said.

"And will they follow this Robak?"

"Oh, yeah," Jace said. "He's a tough one, Robak is. They'll follow him like sheep."

"How tough is he?" Clint asked.

"Well, he's killed men before, I know that."

"How?"

"I seen him."

"Okay," Clint said. "So if we take care of Robak, the others will fall into line."

"Yes, sir."

"All right," Clint said, "now tell me about Jenny Thane."

17

Jace Cole's face melted as he said sincerely, "She's the prettiest woman in town."

Clint figured that. It had been hard not to notice her pale skin, her blue eyes, the long hair that was piled on top of her head right now. She had a long graceful neck, and beneath her simple cotton dress was a firm, womanly body. No, it wasn't hard to believe that she was the prettiest woman in town—but that hadn't been what Clint meant.

"I can believe that," Clint said, "but I meant tell me about her family."

"Oh, well, her father, Daniel Thane, founded Thanesville. He sent her off to the east to get her education, but by the time she got back he'd died. Her ma died even before she left. When she got back ready to be Doc Beacham's nurse, she had no family left."

"I heard her call the mayor 'Uncle.'"

"He ain't her real uncle," Jace said. "He was just friends with her pa, promised he'd look out for her. Same for Doc Beacham. They both promised. I think that's why Doc got her out of town—not that we can't use her right here in Safetown."

"I'm sure you can," Clint said. "Tell me, where's this Robak now?"

"Oh, he's around."

"Are there enough horses for him and his cronies to ride out on?"

"We got lots of horses," Jace said. "The critters weren't affected by the sickness."

"Okay, then you better show me where the horses are."

"Yessir," Jace said. "Right this way."

* * *

Jace took Clint to where the horses were picketed. There were only around thirty of them, so there was no danger of a hundred people mounting up and riding out of Safetown.

"Who handles the horses?"

"Dale Jacks," Jace said. "He was the liveryman in town, so he does the same thing here."

Clint didn't see Eclipse among the horses, and said so.

"Dale would have put your animal separate," Jace said.

"Let's find him."

"Dale?"

"My horse. I want my rifle and saddlebags, and I want to make sure he's being cared for."

"Dale knows what he's doin'," Jace said. "Come on. We'll find him."

They found Dale Jacks having his lunch, but he put his plate down and immediately took Clint to where he'd picketed Eclipse, away from the other horses. He was a short, stocky man in his fifties. He had the gnarled, scarred hands of a man who'd been dealing with the sharp, gnashing teeth of horses most of his life.

"They say this sickness don't affect the horses," he said to Clint, "but I figured, why take a chance with a handsome animal like this one? I decided to keep him away from the others."

"I appreciate it."

Clint saw his saddle leaning against the base of a tree. He went over and liberated his rifle, saddlebags and bedroll.

"You can go back to your meal now," Clint told Dale Jacks. "I've got what I needed."

"I'll take good care of your horse, Mister Adams," Jacks said. "That's a promise."

"I know you will, Mr. Jacks," Clint said. "Thanks."

Clint turned to Jace.

"You better show me where I can bed down."

"Might as well be by me," Jace said. "Come on."

Once again the deputy led the way and Clint followed.

SIX

Ted Robak watched as Jace Cole walked away, leading Clint Adams behind him.

"Now what do we do?" Ned Tyler asked.

Robak didn't answer right away.

"Ted?"

Robak looked at Tyler, who was probably his best friend at the moment. The thought actually made Robak depressed. He had to get out of here, away from Thanesville, and Safetown, and this sickness that was killing everybody.

"We do what we planned on doing," Robak said. "We get the hell away from here."

"But how? We waited too long, if you ask me. We only had the deputy and some storekeepers to deal with, but now they got help from the Gunsmith. I ain't lookin' to tangle with him, Ted."

Robak gave Tyler an angry look.

"Are you lookin' to stay here and die?"

"Well, n-no—"

"I'd rather die by a bullet than the way these poor

bastards are dying," Robak said. "Wouldn't you?"

"Well—"

"You wanna be puking your guts up and go blind and waste away?" Robak asked.

"Hell, no."

"Neither do the others."

"You really think we can count on them now that Adams is here?" Tyler asked.

Robak angrily ground out the cigarette he'd been smoking and turned to face Tyler.

"I guess there's only one way to find out."

"How's that?" Tyler asked with a frown.

"Ask 'em, damn it!" Robak said. Jesus, he had to get away from here so he wouldn't have an idiot as a best friend. "Come on, let's go and find the rest of them."

The rest of them were also idiots, Robak thought, men who had to be told that they should get away from here. They were willing to sit here and wait to die until he started talking to them. A few of them were sure to want to back down when they heard that Clint Adams was here. Robak was going to have to think of some ways to keep them in line. He was good with a gun, but he wasn't in the class of somebody like Clint Adams. What he was, though, was smart, and that was how he was going to have to approach this, with his brain.

SEVEN

After Clint had stowed his bedroll and saddlebags near where Deputy Jace Cole had his, he went looking for some coffee. He found a fire with a pot on it, and an older woman was tending it.

"My name is Sara Connell," she said, handing him his cup.

"Sarah, do you have family in town?"

"I don't have any family," she said. "I used to think that was a bad thing, but most of the people with families had to stay in town with them. I mean, if I had a husband and children, I wouldn't want to leave them, but then I wouldn't have been allowed to."

"How do you mean?"

"Once one family member shows symptoms, the rest were not allowed to leave."

"I see."

"So being a widow, and having been barren the years I was married, will probably end up saving my life."

"You seem optimistic."

She put her hands on her hips and said, "Well, the

simple fact of the matter is, I don't get sick. I mean, I don't even catch a cold, so I got no reason to think I'll catch this . . . whatever it is."

"And what is it?"

"You'll have to ask Jenny that," Sarah said, "but to tell the truth, I don't think that she and Doc even know what it is. Scary, huh?"

"Very," Clint said. "Thanks for the coffee, Ma'am. It's real good."

"I know how to make trail coffee," she said.

"You sure do."

"Let me refill that before you go walkin' off," she said, and after she had done so she added, "and don't forget to bring that cup back. I got to boil it with the rest."

"Yes, Ma'am."

Clint left the fire and walked around the camp, looking for Jenny Thane. He knew the smart thing to do was to mount up and ride out and leave these people to handle this thing by themselves, but every time he thought about doing that an image of that poor devil lying in the grave among the putrid, rancid bodies came to him, and he got angry all over again. A man's life ought to end with more dignity than that.

"You look serious."

He turned and saw Jenny Thane coming up behind him. Behind her he saw a woman with two small children walking away.

"How many children are here?" he asked.

"Not many," she said, brushing a strand of hair away from her face. One or two stuck to her forehead, matted there by perspiration. "Most of them are still in town.

In fact, most of the people here are those without families."

"I was just talking to Mrs. Connell about that," Clint said. "It seems as if a death sentence for one family member is a death sentence for all."

"Unfortunately," she said, "that is the case. Would you walk back to my tent with me?"

"Of course."

As they started to walk, she said to him, "Do you want some free advice?"

"Free advice is always good."

"Ride on," she said. "Get on your horse and keep going."

"You people need help."

"The kind of help we need you can't give us."

"I can try."

"Why?"

He told her what he'd been thinking just before she came along.

"You're a good man."

"I had to kill a helpless man," he said. "I don't know how good that was, but it isn't something I can just walk away from."

"Can you tell me more about the man?"

Clint didn't have to try very hard to bring the man's image to mind again, and he told her what he could.

"Dear God," she said, "that sounds like Matt Foley. He was a member of the town council."

"A friend?"

"No," she said, "I don't have many friends in town."

"But your father founded the town."

"That doesn't matter to me," she said. "I'm friends

with Uncle Horace and with Doc because they were friends with my father."

"No female friends?"

"No," she said. "I'm not married." As if that explained it.

"No male friends?"

"No," she said. "Slim pickings. Besides, I'm much too busy for that kind of nonsense."

They stopped right outside her tent.

"You need some rest," he said. "You look like you're going to collapse."

"How much rest do you think Doc is getting?"

Just then they heard the sound of shots, just a few, and then they died out.

"The sound drifts up here from town," she said. "Probably somebody trying to leave . . . or somebody needing to be put out of their misery."

"Why would they not have done that for Matt Foley?" he asked.

"I don't know," she said. "I can't figure that out. It's something I'm going to ask Doc tomorrow afternoon."

"Don't forget," Clint said, "that I want to go with you."

"I won't," she said. "I think I'm going to try to get that rest you prescribed. Thank you for what you're doing, and what you've done . . . and what you'll probably have to do if you stay."

"I'm staying," he said.

She touched his arm and then turned and went into her tent. He wondered if these people realized how much they owed her.

EIGHT

Deputy Cole entered the tent that belonged to Mayor Horace Russell. Inside he found the mayor, Sam Evers and the third council member, Arnold Pittman.

"So?" Russell asked.

"He's bedded down near me."

"Is he going to be helpful?" Russell asked.

"Very. I wouldn't be able to stop Robak and the others by myself, Mayor," the young lawman said.

"You would have us to help," Pittman said.

"Excuse me for saying so, Mr. Pittman," Cole said, "but you wouldn't be much help, not against Ted Robak."

"How would you—"

"He's right, Arnold," Russell said. "We're three shopkeepers with rifles. We're not going to scare anybody."

"The Gunsmith is," Evers said.

"That's right," the mayor said.

"Is he going to want money?" Pittman asked. "We can't pay him, you know. Not in our present situation. Every penny I have is in the bank."

"All of our assets are in town, Arnold," Russell said.

"I can't allow them to be burned," Pittman said. "Not my money, not everything I own."

"We know that," Horace Russell said. "We all feel the same way."

"That man," Evers said, "the one Adams said he killed?"

Russell looked at him and said, "Matt Foley."

"Yes."

"Jesus," Pittman said. "That's the first one of us to die."

"Yes," Russell said.

"Why would they throw him in that grave alive?" Evers wondered.

"Maybe," Mayor Russell said, "somebody was trying to send us a message."

"I don't understand that," Deputy Cole said. "What kind of message?"

Russell looked at Cole.

"You don't have to understand, Jace," Russell said. "Just make sure you do your job."

"A job I'm not getting paid for anymore."

"You'll be paid," Russell said, "don't worry."

"Yeah," Cole said, and backed out of the tent.

"Is he gonna hold up?" Pittman asked.

"He'll do fine," Russell said, "and he'll do what he's told."

"What about Jenny?" Pittman asked.

"Leave Jenny alone," Russell said, with heat in his tone. "Do you both understand?"

"We understand, Horace," Evers said.

"Then get out," Russell said. "I've got some thinking to do."

"About what?" Pittman asked.

"About how to save everything we've worked for," the mayor said. "Everything that we've built."

"You mean everything Jenny's father built," Evers said, "don't you?"

Russell's eyes narrowed to slits and he said to Evers, "Get out, Sam."

"Come on, Sam," Pittman said, grabbing the other man's arm. "We'd better go."

He tugged Evers outside.

"Why does he get a tent?" Evers asked.

"He's the mayor."

"Any one of us could be the mayor."

"But we chose Horace, didn't we?" Pittman said.

"Yes," Evers said, "and I often wonder if we made the right choice."

They began to walk away from the tent.

"One of us is dead now," Evers pointed out.

"I know."

"There's only six left."

"I know that, Sam."

"What are we gonna do?"

"What can we do?" Pittman asked. "We have to sit and wait, like everybody else."

"Maybe," Evers said, "but I ain't waitin' forever."

"None of us are, Sam."

It was about twenty minutes later when Jenny Thane appeared at the flap of Horace Russell's tent.

"Are you awake, Uncle?"

"Come in, Jenny," Russell said, sitting up on his roughly made cot. "You're supposed to be resting, dear."

"I tried," she said. "I can't sleep."

"What's on your mind?"

"You mean besides everybody dying around us?" she asked. "Clint Adams."

"What about him?"

"He doesn't know what he's getting himself into," she said. "You've got to persuade him to leave, Uncle Horace."

"Jenny," Russell said, "he wants to help, and quite frankly, we need it. Robak and his cronies are going to bolt any minute now. If they do that they could carry this illness all over the Southwest."

"I know, but—"

"We have to measure the risk of one man against the risk of many, child," Horace Russell said. "I'm afraid it's no contest."

"I suppose."

"He interests you, this man?"

She did not tell her uncle that her thoughts, as she tried to rest, had kept straying to Clint Adams. The way he stood, the way he tilted his head, the way his mouth looked . . . she had not had thoughts like this about a man in a very long time . . . and this was the wrong time for it.

"I have no time for that."

"You should be married, Jenny."

"I know," she said, "I'm not getting any younger." She laughed. "I doubt that this particular man is marriage material, Uncle."

"No," Russell said, "I don't suppose that he is. Go

back to your tent, Jenny. Even if you can't sleep, let your body rest."

"Yes, all right."

He grabbed her hand and said, "We could not get though this without you."

"Yes," she said, "you would."

She wanted to kiss his cheek, but even the touch of his hand was a risk, she knew. All of them were being very careful not to touch, and a kiss—no matter how innocent—would be even worse.

"I'll see you later, Uncle," she said, and left.

Horace Russell had a lot to think about. Matt Foley's death was a shock. None of the seven was supposed to die. It was not good for the remaining six. They each had knowledge the others needed.

And Robak. What the hell was he thinking? Once the man had worked for him, but now he was out of control.

And then there was Jenny. He'd promised her father that he would look after her, but if she found out . . . if she got in the way . . . he shook his head. He didn't want to think of that at all.

And now the presence of Clint Adams. Initially he would be a help, especially to young Cole, but what about later?

And his own cronies, Evers and Pittman. They were becoming nervous enough to do something foolish.

All of these things ran through his mind and he wondered why, with all of that, this terrible disease had to come along. What was it? How long would it last? Would it wipe them all out completely? Only Doc Beacham stood between them and the disease. What if something happened to him? What if it had been him who Clint Adams had found in that grave?

Russell laid down on his cot and tried to do what he had advised Jenny to do. He knew he wouldn't sleep, but at least this way his body would rest.

NINE

Later that night, Ned Tyler found Ted Robak sitting by a fire, drinking coffee. He got himself a cup, poured it full and sat down next to Robak.

"What?" Robak said.

"I thought you might be interested in hearing what I just heard," Tyler said.

"And what's that?"

"Jenny Thane is going to meet with Doc Beacham tomorrow."

"So? She does that a couple of times a week."

"Yeah," Tyler said, with satisfaction, "but this time Clint Adams is gonna be going with her."

Robak looked at Tyler.

"Yeah," Tyler said, "I thought you'd find that interesting."

"Go get the rest of the boys," Robak said. "We got some things to talk about."

"What, now?"

"Right now."

Tyler looked longingly down at the cup of coffee in

his hand, then dumped it on the ground, put the cup down and got up to go and find the others.

The others consisted of six more men whom Robak had convinced that the only way to stay alive was to get away from Thanesville and Safetown. Of the six, Robak felt he could count on at least two of them to back any play he made. They were Vince Mann and Frank Hunter. Both were men like Robak, drifters who made their way any way they could, sometimes with a gun. They had just happened to find themselves in Thanesville during this epidemic.

The other four were men who lived in town, had no families, who worked at odd jobs and would not be leaving all that much behind. At least, that's what Robak convinced them of. In the event of gunplay, though, he wasn't all that sure that they would stand up—especially against the Gunsmith.

Tyler managed to find them all and brought them to Robak's camp, which he had pitched some distance away from Safetown, for privacy.

Robak had put a fresh pot of coffee on, enough for all eight of them. When they were all there, and all had cups, he told them his plan.

"We move tomorrow," he said.

"Why tomorrow?" Hunter asked.

"You probably all heard who rode into Safetown today?"

"I heard it was Clint Adams," Mann said.

"That's right," Robak said.

"So, with Adams here to stand with the deputy," one of the others asked nervously, "how do you expect us to make a move?"

"Jenny Thane is going to go and meet with Doc Beacham tomorrow," Robak explained.

"So?" somebody said. "She does that all the time."

"This time," Robak said, without giving Tyler credit for having found this out, "Adams is going with her."

A few of the men sat up straighter when they heard this.

"So while he's away," Hunter said, "we ride out."

"Right," Robak said.

"The deputy will try to stop us," Mann said.

"I know."

"Well, what do we do then?" one of the others asked.

"We handle it," Robak said.

"Kill him?"

"I'd rather do this without killing him," Robak said. "If we kill him, we'll be wanted."

"So what do we do?"

"We take him by surprise," Robak said, "get his gun away from him and get the hell away from here."

"I'm for that," Hunter said.

"Me, too," Tyler said.

And one by one all of the others chimed in with their agreement to the plan.

TEN

Jenny came and got Clint after lunch the next day.

"Time to go," she said, "if you're coming."

"I'm coming," he said.

"I'll get my horse and meet you by my tent," she said.

"Right."

Clint went and got Eclipse, saddled him and rode him over to Jenny's tent. She was waiting with a little sway-backed bay mare who wouldn't get her very far. Luckily, she didn't have far to go.

"How long before we get back?" he asked her.

"I guess that depends on how much Doc has to say," she replied. "Probably no more than two hours."

Clint looked at Deputy Cole.

"Hold the fort that long, boy."

"Yessir."

Jenny turned her horse, and Clint moved Eclipse to follow her. Before they could get very far, though, their way was blocked by Mayor Horace Russell.

"You be careful, Jenny," he said, grabbing her horse's head. "Be real careful out there."

"I'm meeting Doc, Uncle Horace," she said. "I've done it many times before, and I've got Clint with me this time."

"Just be on the lookout," Russell said, looking past her directly at Clint, who was wondering what the man expected to happen.

"We will, Uncle," she said. She gave a little tug on her reins, and Russell released her horse. "We will."

She started off again, and Clint followed, still wondering what Horace Russell was afraid of.

Tyler came running over to Robak's fire, where Robak was sitting, having another cup of coffee. Seems all he did was sit around and wait and drink coffee. He was tired of waiting.

"Well?" he asked.

"They're gone," Tyler said, "just rode out."

"How long?"

"I heard her say two hours."

"Plenty of time," Robak said, dumping the remnants of his coffee into the fire. "Let's go."

"So tell me," Clint said to Jenny, "what does Doc Beacham think this illness is?"

"He doesn't know," she replied. "That's what's so frustrating."

"Has he called for outside help?"

"He's afraid to," she said. "he doesn't want to take a chance on it spreading."

"That doesn't make sense," Clint said. "For this kind of thing there's got to be somebody who can help."

"Doc's a real good doctor."

"That may be," Clint said, "but he's still a small-time

doctor. I'm sure if he got in touch with the government they'd send somebody who could help."

"Do you think?"

"Yes, I do," Clint said.

"I guess Doc doesn't think so," she said. "And he's pretty much right all the time."

"People are dying, Jenny," Clint said. "How right could he be?"

"You don't know Doc," Jenny said. "He's got reasons for everything he does."

"Well," Clint said, "I'll be real interested to hear his reasons for this."

They reached the clearing first and dismounted. The day was hot. Clint removed his canteen from his saddle and offered it to Jenny.

"No," she said, "I have my own."

Clint shrugged, took a drink and returned the canteen to his saddle.

"While you're here, Clint," she said, "get used to not sharing anything of yours. Don't let anyone else drink out of your canteen."

"I thought everyone in Safetown was . . . well, safe?"

"I check everyone twice a day for symptoms."

"Find anyone yet?"

"No."

"What will you do when you do find someone?"

"Send them back to town, I guess."

"So they can end up in that grave?" Clint asked. "Is that Doc's idea, too? That mass grave?"

"He thinks we should keep them all together."

"And what about burying them?"

"We'll do that, soon," she said. "When it's all over."

"Just one big grave, huh?"

"Or maybe burn them," she said. "It might be safer that way."

"I just hope before somebody tosses a match in there," Clint said, "they make sure that they're all dead."

"Here he comes," Jenny said.

ELEVEN

A buckboard approached the clearing, and Clint could see a man the same age as Horace Russell driving it. He was in shirtsleeves, with white hair that covered about half his head. He stopped the buckboard and climbed down, almost painfully. As he approached them on foot, Clint could see that he looked completely exhausted.

"You don't look good, Doc," Jenny said.

"I'm fine," the man said. "Just tired."

"No symptoms yet?" she asked.

"No, Jenny," he said, "no symptoms yet, thank God. Would you introduce me to your friend? And tell me what the hell he's doing here?"

"Doc Beacham, this is Clint Adams," Jenny said. "Clint, this is Doc."

"Doc," Clint said, making no move to shake hands or close the twenty-foot gap between them.

"Clint Adams, the Gunsmith?" Doc asked.

"That's right," Jenny said.

"When did he get here?"

"Just yesterday."

41

"Does he know what's going on?"

"I'm right here, Doctor," Clint said, "and yes, I do know what's going on."

"I'm sorry," the doctor said, running his hand through his already unruly shock of white hair, "I didn't mean . . . you should leave this area."

"I was given to understand that the people in Safetown were . . . well, safe."

"No one is safe," the doctor said. "This thing is in the air, Mr. Adams."

"What?" Jenny said, shocked. "What are you talking about? You don't have to touch someone to pass it on?"

"Apparently not," Doc Beacham said.

"B-but . . . how can that be?" Jenny asked.

"Doc," Clint said, "are you saying that this . . . disease is going to spread all over the country and there's nothing we can do about it?"

"I honestly don't know," Beacham said. "It can be passed by touch but apparently doesn't have to be. However, I don't know the range of the thing."

"You mean, it may not be able to travel far in the air?" Clint asked. "It might . . . what, lose its potency?"

"It's possible."

"You're telling me what's possible, Doctor," Clint said, "how about telling me what's probable?"

"Mr. Adams," Doc Beacham said, "it's probable that we're all going to die. That's why you must leave."

"What if I'm carrying it already?"

"I—I don't know—"

"Then I can't very well leave, can I?" Clint asked. "And neither can anyone else."

"No."

"What about you, Doc?" Clint asked. "Why don't you have it?"

"It's poss—I may be immune," Doc Beacham said. "Some of us may well be immune."

"What about the sheriff?" Clint asked. "He's an old friend of mine. I was coming here to see him. How is he?"

"As of now Sheriff Ives is fine," Doc said. "He might be immune as well."

"Doc," Jenny said, "Mr. Adams found Matt Foley. He—he was still alive, lying in that . . . that pit . . ."

"That wasn't my doing . . ." the doctor said, shaking his head.

"Whose was it?" she asked.

Beacham looked at Clint, then looked away.

"It was Ives."

"What?" Clint said. "I don't believe it."

"He thought Foley was dead and wanted him out of town," Beacham said.

"But didn't you know that he was alive?" Jenny asked.

"I was tending to someone else at the time, Jenny," Beacham said. "By the time I knew anything had happened they'd already removed Foley from town. I didn't know he was still alive."

Clint wasn't sure Beacham was telling the whole truth. He simply couldn't believe that Henry Ives would make a mistake like that.

"How are all your people, Jenny?" Doc Beacham asked.

"I check them every day like you told me, Doc," she said, "twice a day. They seem fine, so far."

"Good, good," Beacham said. "I have to get back."

"How many more . . . are sick, Doc?"

Beacham took a deep breath, let it out slowly and then said, "I expect to lose six more by morning."

"So there's no sign of it letting up?" Clint asked.

"No sign."

"Are any of them children, Doc?" Jenny asked.

"Jenny, dear—"

"Are they?"

"Yes."

Jenny lowered her head.

"Mr. Adams," Beacham said, "if you're going to be around, I hope you'll be helping young Jason Cole with his job."

"I'll be helping him."

"Good, good," Beacham said. "If anyone gets it into their heads to leave Safetown, they'll have to be stopped."

"Don't worry, Doc," Clint said, "We'll stop them, you just worry about stopping this disease."

"It's all I've *been* thinking about, Mr. Adams," Beacham said, "believe me."

TWELVE

They watched Doc Beacham painfully climb aboard his buggy and drive away before Clint made a move to remount. As he put his hands on Eclipse, he wished he had asked Doc if this disease was affecting animals at all.

"Clint?"

'He turned and looked at Jenny.

"Can we wait here a few minutes before going back?"

"Sure," he said, backing away from Eclipse. "Whatever you want, Jenny."

She looked at the sky and folded her arms, hugging herself as if she was cold.

"It's just . . . I need a few minutes before I . . . go back there . . ."

"I understand."

"Do you?"

"Well," he admitted, "probably not."

"They're all depending on me," she said. "Growing up in Thanesville I saw the way people depended on my father, and on Doc, and I thought it must be wonderful,

45

but now . . . now they're depending on me."

"Jenny, it's perfectly natural to feel like wilting under this kind of pressure," he said.

"Is it?"

"Look at Doc Beacham," Clint said. "He was wilting."

She looked at him and asked, "Was he?"

"He sure looked wilted to me," Clint said. "Disheveled, confused . . ."

Jenny smiled an affectionate smile and said, "Clint, Doc always looks disheveled and confused, but beneath all of that is a brilliant mind."

"Well then, there's no way that you should be trying to compare yourself to him," Clint said. "I get the feeling he's been a hero to you all your life, since you were a child."

"A hero," she said, "a second father . . ."

"Then there's certainly no way you're ever going to measure up," he said. "You might as well not even try."

"You're right, of course," she said. Her face became grim. "I guess I'm just tired of trying. There doesn't seem to be anything that we can do to . . . to stop this thing."

"Jenny, have any animals been affected?"

"What?"

"Horses? Dogs? Any others that you know of?"

She frowned and said, "No, I don't believe so. Are you worried about your horse?"

"Well," Clint said, stroking the big Arabian's neck, "I haven't had him that long, but have you and Doc considered whether animals have some kind of immunity to this disease?"

"Animals," she said, "and some humans."

"Maybe if you could find out what they have in common you could come up with a way to fight it."

She turned to face him.

"That's so simple it's brilliant!"

"Well . . . when can we pass this brilliant idea on to Doc?"

"We'll meet here again in two days, same time," she said.

"Not until then? Isn't there a way to get a message to him?"

"Not unless someone is willing to ride into town with it."

"Someone in Safetown must be immune."

"But who?" she asked. "Who's immune, and who has simply not gotten the disease yet?"

"I see your point," he said. "Well, then I guess we'll just have to wait two days to talk to Doc again."

She rubbed her face with her hands, then dropped them to her side as if they weighed a ton.

"I guess we'd better get back," she said.

"Are you all right?"

"I'll be fine," she said. "Every once in a while I just need to go somewhere alone and feel sorry for myself. Thanks for listening."

"No problem."

He had the feeling he should hold her just for a moment or two, but the time for that passed, and they mounted their horses and headed back.

THIRTEEN

Henry Ives looked out the window at the street below. Normally, the main street of Thanesville would be bustling with activity at this time of day. Today, like every day the past few weeks, it was empty. Those who hadn't left to go to Safetown were in their homes, as if they thought they could hide there from this hideous disease that was killing their town.

Henry Ives was a lawman. He was used to dealing with danger he could see, hear and touch. All he could see of this disease was what it left behind. He couldn't fight what he couldn't see. This battle was being fought by Doc Beacham and by Jenny Thane, so what good was he and his badge?

"Henry?"

He turned, looked at lovely Hannah Lowell lying in her bed. He and Hannah had been circling each other for years. The only good thing about this disease was that it had finally driven them into each other's arms. Neither of them wanted to die without telling the other how they felt, and without acting on their feelings.

Ives was in his forties, Hannah in her early thirties. One of the reasons he had never approached her—no matter how friendly they appeared to have gotten—was because he couldn't imagine that she'd feel the same way he did. He'd been afraid of rejection.

"Come to bed, Henry."

She was naked, her body pale and almost glowing in the light from the window. She was a full-bodied woman, with broad hips, wide shoulders, and heavy breasts with dark brown nipples. Her hair was brown and long, long enough to almost hide those big, beautiful breasts.

The first time he'd held them in his hands and kissed them, taken the nipples into his mouth and rolled them with his tongue, he'd thought himself the luckiest man alive. Later, he felt guilty about it, for people all around him were dying. But looking at her now, naked, her arms held out to him, he knew that if he died tomorrow, at least he'd had this time with her, and that did make him very lucky.

He walked to the bed, as naked as she, and got into it with her. He gathered her up into his arms, pulled the sheet up over them, and held her tightly. Her skin was as hot as ever. He was worried about that. The first indication of the disease, according to Doc, was fever.

Ives didn't know—and Doc didn't know—why they had not been hit with the disease yet. Hannah confided to him that she prayed every night, prayed that even if everyone in town died that they would live and be together. She was worried that this was some kind of sin, but she didn't care. Now that they'd found each other she didn't want them to die—and it would have been worse if only one of them did. That would leave the other alone, all alone after they had found each other.

He moved his hands over her, enjoying the smoothness of her skin. She slid her hand down over his belly, down between his legs where she took him in her hand and stroked him. As he swelled to her touch he felt both pleasure and guilt. He was the law in this town, the man everyone turned to for help when things went wrong, but he and his badge were not doing anyone any good these days. And so here he was, lying in bed with Hannah, enjoying the smell of her, the feel and taste of her, while people around them died.

"It's not out fault," she said.

"What?"

"It's not our fault that people are dying and we're not," she said. "There's nothing wrong with us loving each other and feeling lucky that we're together."

"You're reading my mind," he said.

"I've been reading your mind for years, Henry Ives," she said. She straddled him then, pinning his erection between them, and stared down at him. "Can you read my mind, now?"

"I don't have to," he said, reaching for her breasts and bringing them to his mouth, "I can read your body."

"Oh," she said, as his tongue touched her nipples, "and what's it saying to you?"

He answered, but his face was buried between her breasts and she couldn't make out the words. It didn't matter, though. She lifted her hips and he slid into her easily because she was wet now, and their bodies were doing all the talking . . .

"What about your friend?" she asked later.

"Clint?"

"Yes," he said. "Didn't his telegram say he was coming here?"

"Yes."

"How do we keep him away?"

"I don't know," Ives said. "I don't know where he is, so I can't warn him. I guess I'll just have to be on the lookout for him."

"Henry," she asked, "when are we going to send for help?"

"When Doc says, I guess," Ives answered. "Doc's in charge right now, Hannah."

"But you're the law."

"This is out of my league," he said. "I don't know what to do about this situation. I feel . . . useless."

She snuggled up against him and said, "Not to me, you don't."

He held her tight and said, "I'm surprised that something this good could have come out of something this bad."

FOURTEEN

When they got back to Safetown it was clear something had gone wrong—very, very wrong. The general attitude in the camp was one of great distress. People were milling about, and there was a group of them in front of Horace Russell's tent.

"What's going on?" Jenny asked.

"I think we better find out."

They dismounted and approached the group in front of the mayor's tent.

"What happened here?" Jenny asked aloud.

The crowd of people parted, and she and Clint could see, sitting in their midst, Jace Cole being tended to by Sarah Connell and watched closely by Horace Russell. Cole was bleeding from the head.

"What happened?" Clint asked.

"Robak," Russell said. "He and his boys pistol-whipped Jace, took their horses and rode out."

"I tried to stop 'em," Cole said, "but there was too many."

Clint frowned. Obviously Robak had decided that

53

Clint's appearance in camp meant he should make his move. Once he realized that Clint had gone to see Doc Beacham with Jenny, he probably figured they should move immediately before he got back.

"How many?" Clint asked.

"Six, altogether," Russell said.

"I better get after them," Clint said. "Which way did they—"

"I'm going, too—" Cole said, trying to rise, but Sarah Connell was insistent that he let her finish bandaging his head.

"You'll bleed to death otherwise," she finished.

"Wait for me," Cole said to Clint.

"You might as well stay behind, Jace—"

"It's my job, Adams," Cole said, "not yours."

"And you didn't do it very well," Sam Evers chimed in.

Jenny turned on him and said, "I'd like to see you stand up to six men. As a matter of fact, where were you when this happened?"

"It's not my job to stop them," Evers said.

"It's everyone's job," Clint said. "If they carry this disease to a densely populated area a lot of people could die. This could become an epidemic if we don't stop it right here and now."

As soon as Sarah finished his bandage, Jace Cole stood up.

"I'm ready to go when you are, Clint."

"All right, Jace," Clint said. "Let's go."

"Some of you other men should go with them," Jenny called out. "Are you all a bunch of cowards?"

"We're storekeepers, Jenny," Horace Russell said. "Not gunmen."

"If you were any kind of men," Jenny said, speaking to them all in general, "you'd ride out of here with them."

Clint and Jason didn't wait to hear the outcome. Clint walked Eclipse over to where the horses were picketed so Deputy Cole could saddle his horse, and then they both mounted up. There was still a crowd of people in front of Mayor Russell's tent, but they ignored them. Before they could ride out, though, Sarah Connell came running over, carrying a burlap sack.

"You won't be able to stop anywhere for supplies," she said. "Here's some jerky and dried fruit, in case you have to stay out overnight."

"Thank you, Sarah," Clint said, accepting the bag and hanging it from his saddle. "We'll be back as soon as we can."

"Godspeed," she said. "Jenny's right. The rest of these men are just cowards."

"They're all better off here, Sarah," Clint said. "The more of us there are riding around out there, the more chance there is of spreading this disease."

"They're still cowards," Jenny said, coming up behind Sarah.

"You hold the fort here, Jenny," Clint said, "and if we're not back in two days remember what you were going to tell Doc Beacham."

"I remember, Clint," Jenny said. "Hurry back."

Clint nodded, and he and Cole rode out.

According to Jace Cole, Robak and his men rode out of camp going west.

"I don't know if they'll keep on going that way, though," the deputy said.

"We'll just have to track them," Clint said.

"I—I can't track," the deputy admitted. "I don't know how."

"I can track."

"Really? You're an expert?"

"No," Clint said, "but I'm good enough to track this bunch. Tell me what happened back there, Jace."

"Robak fronted me, said him and his boys were leavin'," Cole said. "Before I knew it one of them had me from behind. Robak took out his gun. I thought he was gonna kill me, but he just clubbed me. When I come to they was gone. I—I really messed up, Clint."

"Don't worry about it, Jace," Clint said. "We'll catch them."

"And bring them back?"

"If we can."

"And if we can't bring 'em back?"

"We can't let them possibly carry this disease to another town, Jace," Clint said, "or to a city."

"We'll kill 'em?"

"If we have to," Clint said. He looked over at the younger man. "Are you up for that?"

"I'll do my job, Clint," Cole said. "Whatever it takes."

"Okay, then," Clint said, "let's start tracking."

FIFTEEN

They picked up the trail left by the six men fairly easily and followed it at a good clip.

"What about supplies?" Clint asked.

"I didn't have time to check," Cole said.

"Well, if they were planning this they'd have to have some supplies stashed away somewhere," Clint said. "They're going to camp sometimes. That's probably when we'll catch up to them." Clint looked at the sky. "It'll be dark soon."

"Should we stop for the night?" Cole asked.

"No," Clint said, "we can't afford to stop. We'll keep moving in the dark. We'll catch up to them faster that way."

"You can track them in the dark?"

"Believe me," Clint said, "by the time it's dark we'll know where they've camped.

It was a couple of hours later, in the dark, when Clint called a halt to their progress.

"What is it?" the deputy asked.

"Don't you smell it?"

"Smell what?" Cole sniffed the air. "I don't smell—wait a minute."

"There it is, huh?"

Cole sniffed the air again and then brightened. "Coffee?"

"Right," Clint said. "Coffee. Now all we have to do is follow our noses."

Several minutes later he called a halt to their progress once again and whispered, "Dismount and secure your horse."

"What are we doin'?" Cole whispered back.

"We'll approach on foot," Clint said. "Either our horses or theirs would give us away, otherwise. Come on."

Cole drew his gun, and Clint put his hand out with the palm facing down.

"Put it away," Clint said. "We won't need it yet." He didn't want the young deputy squeezing off a round by accident if he took a bad step. He waited for Cole to holster the weapon, then led the way.

When they came within sight of the camp, Clint signalled for Cole to get down on his belly next to him. As they watched, four men were sitting around a campfire, drinking coffee and making too much noise for men who were on the run.

"I don't see Robak," Cole said. "Or Ned Tyler."

"They must have split up," Clint said. "We've been following the trail of these four. Damn it! I should have seen it if they had split before this."

"Maybe they split up right here?"

"It's possible," Clint said, only slightly mollified.

"So what do we do now?" Cole asked. "Wait until morning?"

"No," Clint said.

"Why not? They're not going anywhere."

"They have coffee," Clint said, "and we don't. I'm not going to sit out here all night while they sit by a fire and drink coffee."

"So we're gonna go in and get them now?"

Clint nodded, rolled onto his back and looked at the deputy.

"That's right, Jace," he said, "we're going to go in and get them . . . right now."

Clint explained his quickly formulated plan to Jace and then told him to stay where he was until he worked his way around to the other side of the camp.

"Why don't they have somebody on watch?" Cole asked.

"We'll ask them after we've taken them, Jace," Clint said as he moved into the darkness.

Jace Cole waited nervously, counting to a hundred the way Clint Adams had told him to. He also kept his gun in his holster until they were ready to move. This was something else Clint had told him. No point in squeezing off a hasty or nervous shot before they were ready. Cole did not take offense at these "suggestions." True, he was the one wearing the badge, but he didn't have nearly as much experience as Clint Adams did. He was very willing to let Clint be in charge. In fact, Cole couldn't wait for all of this disease stuff to be over so he could go back to being Henry Ives's deputy, with his only re-

sponsibilities being to do whatever the sheriff told him
to do.

He got to his feet but stayed crouched down while he
counted ninety-seven . . . ninety-eight . . . ninety-nine . . .

SIXTEEN

At one hundred, both Clint and Jace Cole charged into the camp with their guns in their hands.

"Nobody move!" Clint yelled.

All four men stood up quickly and went for their guns. Clint had thought he might have to make an example of one man, maybe, but he expected at least three to respond to his command by freezing.

It didn't happen that way.

"Down, Jace!" Clint yelled.

Cole hit the ground as the four men drew their guns. Clint fired and took one man down with a bullet in the hip. Cole fired frantically, pulling the trigger until his gun was empty. He hit one man, putting him down to the ground with a bullet in the head.

The other men were also frantic, and nobody but Clint was thinking clearly. He had one man on the ground with a bullet in his hip, so he decided not to try to be cute with the others. He shot one in the chest and the other in the belly. One of them fell facedown on the campfire and Clint found it odd to find that he was hoping that the pot of coffee that went sprawling, emptying into the dirt, was not the last of it.

He rushed forward and pulled the dead man off the fire before his body would either extinguish it or burst into flames.

Cole got to his feet, his empty gun in his hand.

"Reload!" Clint shouted.

"But they're dead—"

"This one isn't!" Clint yelled, "Reload, damnit. Don't ever stand around with an empty gun."

Hastily, Cole ejected the empties from his gun and replaced them with live rounds.

"Now holster it," Clint said, "and check those two." He pointed at the wounded man. "I'll deal with him."

He walked over to the injured man and leaned over him. His face was screwed up in pain and he had both hands pressed to his hip.

"Hurt?" Clint asked.

"Jesus," the man said, "ya gotta help me . . ."

"Like you were going to help a lot of people die if you're carrying the disease?"

"Man, you gotta help me," the man gasped.

"Yeah, sure," Clint said. He knelt by the man. "Let me see it."

Clint had to yank the man's hands away from his wound. As he did so, he became aware of the knife in the man's hand. It flashed toward him and he just barely avoided it, jerking back and losing his balance. He landed on his right hip, on his gun, as the man—apparently not nearly as incapacitated as he had appeared—lunged at him with the knife.

Clint heard the shot and saw the blood blossom on the man's chest. The force of the bullet drove him backward and then onto his back, where he lay still, and dead.

Clint looked behind him and saw Jace Cole standing there with his gun in his hand.

"Nice shooting, kid," he said. "Thanks."

SEVENTEEN

Clint and Cole dragged the four bodies out into the darkness, and then Clint sent the deputy to collect their horses. By the time Jace returned with the animals, Clint had found the coffee and had another pot on the fire.

They each unsaddled their own horses, cared for them, then sat down at the fire with coffee and some dried jerky.

"Now what do we do?" Cole asked.

"In the morning we'll bury them, and then we'll try to pick up the trail of the other two."

"Why should we bury them?" Cole asked. "Why should we take the time to bury them?"

Clint thought about the man he'd found lying in a mass grave and said, "Because everybody deserves to be buried. I'm not going to leave them out for the scavengers."

Cole didn't seem convinced.

"Besides," Clint added, "if they're carrying the disease, the best place for them is in the ground."

"Well . . . yeah, I guess that's true."

"We'll dig shallow graves and then get under way," Clint said. "It won't take long."

They sat in silence for a while and then Cole said, "If you hadn't made me reload when you did, you might be dead."

"That's true."

"What happened?"

"He wasn't as hurt as he made out," Clint said. "It was only when he pulled the knife out from under him that I saw it in the firelight. I jerked back and fell on my right hip, pinning my gun under me."

"So . . . I saved your life?"

"You sure did," Clint said, "and I appreciate it."

Cole stared into the fire and swallowed.

"First men you ever killed?" Clint asked.

The young man looked at Clint.

"Yeah."

"It won't get any easier," Clint said. "This will help you decide if you want to keep wearing a badge or not."

"I guess."

"Don't look into the fire, Jace," Clint said. "It will ruin your night vision. They were looking into the fire when we charged in, and when they tried to find us they couldn't see properly."

Cole jerked his eyes away from the fire and said, "Oh."

"We'll have to set a watch," Clint said. "I'll take the first."

"No," Cole said, "I'll do it."

"Jace—"

"I couldn't close my eyes right now."

Clint stared across at the kid and then said, "Okay,

Jace. You take the first watch and wake me in four hours."

"Okay."

"I'll just have another cup of coffee before I turn in."

"What are we gonna do with their horses, and their gear?"

"We'll bury their guns with them," Clint said. "We'll just unsaddle the horses and let them loose."

"What about the disease?"

"It doesn't seem to affect animals."

"Oh."

"We'll just leave their saddles and saddlebags behind. Somebody will come along and go through them."

"Why don't we go through them?"

"We will," Clint said, "but just to see if there's anything in them to tell us where Robak's going. We're not going to keep anything."

"Why not?"

"Because I don't rob graves, or the dead, Jace," Clint said, "and it's not a habit you should get into, either."

"Okay."

Clint dumped the remnants of his coffee into the fire and said, "I'm turning in now. Wake me in four hours. Remember."

"I'll remember."

Clint rolled himself up in his blanket, turned his back to the fire, then turned back and said, "And don't think about them out there."

"I won't."

"Don't think about the ones you killed."

"I . . . won't."

"It won't help anything, Jace."

"I know!"

Clint decided to let the boy be and let him deal with it on his own. He rolled over to go to sleep.

Jace Cole couldn't help it.

He was thinking about the dead men lying out in the dark, specifically the two he had killed. Clint was right. He was going to have to decide after this—after all of this—whether or not he wanted to continue to wear a badge for the rest of his life.

If he survived this.

EIGHTEEN

In the morning Clint resisted the urge to put on a pot of coffee. He woke Cole and said, "We got burial duty."

They found some flat stones and used them as shovels to dig four shallow graves and roll the bodies into them. Once they were covered up, still wearing their guns, they unsaddled the four horses and sent them on their way with a slap on their rumps. That done, they settled down to go through the dead men's saddlebags.

"Nothing," Clint said. "Nothing to tell us where Robak might be going, and nothing of value. How about you?" He'd gone through two sets of saddlebags, with Cole going through the other two.

"Nothing here, either," the deputy said.

"All right, then," Clint said, "we're back to tracking then." He stood up, dropped the saddlebags by the saddles and brushed off his hands. Cole stood and did the same.

"Let's get our own animals saddled and put that fire out," Clint said.

Clint kicked the fire to death then saddled Eclipse. By

that time Cole had his horse saddled as well.

"Now what?" Cole asked.

"Let's look for some tracks," Clint said. "If we're lucky, it happened like you said. They all got there and then split up."

Cole remained where he was while Clint moved about the camp, checking the ground.

"Well, well . . ." he said, eventually.

"What?"

"We did get lucky. Look here."

Cole walked over to where Clint was crouched and crouched down next to him.

"Two sets of tracks, moving off to the north."

"Robak and Tyler."

"Has to be," Clint said.

"If they're going north, they're not gonna come to another town real soon," Cole said.

"That's good."

"Unless they rode through the night, too."

"No," Clint said, "they wouldn't."

"Why not?"

"They wouldn't figure they'd have to," Clint said. "They'd know that we'd find these four first. No way we'd be able to keep riding after that."

"So they camped?"

Clint nodded and stood up.

"And they're probably breaking camp right now, like we are."

"So what do we do?"

"That's easy, Jace," Clint said. "We get mounted and ride hell-for-leather after them."

* * *

Robak watched as Ned Tyler stamped the fire out. He stood and looked behind them. By now Adams and the deputy must have caught up to the other four. Robak had been talking to them all the way, getting them worked up, telling them they couldn't let themselves be taken. He wanted them so on edge that they'd go for their guns at the slightest sound. With any luck that's what happened when Adams and Jace Cole caught up to them, and maybe somebody got in a lucky shot. Maybe either the deputy or the Gunsmith was carrying a bullet right now.

"You ready?" Ned Tyler asked.

Robak looked at Tyler.

"I'm ready."

"What are you lookin' at?"

"Nothin'," Robak said. "Just lookin'. Come on, let's get mounted up and move out."

Ives looked up as Doc Beacham entered the sheriff's office.

"Coffee ready?" the older man asked.

"Been ready," Ives said. "Where've you been. Haven't seen you since you went out to see Jenny. How are things out there?"

"About the same," Beacham said, sitting across from the lawman with a cup of coffee. "By the way, I met your friend."

"What friend is that?"

"Clint Adams?"

"He's here?" Ives asked, alarmed.

"He's in Safetown."

Somewhat relieved, Ives asked, "How did he get there?"

Beacham sipped his coffee before answering.

"He found Matt Foley, Henry."

"You mean he found Foley's body? And that mass grave?"

"He found the grave," Beacham said, 'but according to Adams, Matt was still alive."

Dumbstruck, Ives couldn't speak for a few seconds and then all he said was, "What?"

"That's what he said."

"W-what happened? Did he touch him?"

"No," Beacham said, "Matt asked Adams to finish him and, mercifully, he did."

"Doc," Ives said, after a moment, "I swear I thought Matt was dead. I never would have put him out there—"

"I know that, Henry," Beacham said, "I know."

"Did you tell Clint—"

"Yes, I told him that."

"Has he gone?"

"No," Beacham said, "apparently he's agreed to stay in Safetown and help young Jace."

"Well," Ives said, "Jace does need help, but I wish Clint would have just moved on."

"He realized that once he came into contact with the people in Safetown he couldn't, Henry," Beacham said. "Not until this is all over, anyway."

Henry Ives rubbed his face.

"My God," he said, behind his hands, "poor Matt . . ."

"You didn't know, Henry."

Ives dropped his hands.

"I should have known, Doc," he said. "That's my job. I'm supposed to know when a man is dead. I guess I . . . I just didn't examine him close enough."

Beacham remained silent.

"I guess I'd better leave that up to you from now on."

"That sounds like a good idea."

Ives sat back and touched the silver star on his chest.

"I don't know what good I'm doing anyone, anymore, Doc," he said. "I'm just . . . taking up space around here."

"That's nonsense and you know it, Henry."

"Do I?"

"Yes," Doc said, "you do."

Doc put his empty coffee mug on the desk and stood up. "Let's not start feeling sorry for ourselves, Henry. That's the last thing we need to do."

"You're right, Doc," Ives said. "I know that."

"I've got to make my rounds," Doc Beacham said, heading for the door.

"Well," Ives said, "at this point Clint is reasonably safe out there. Safer than if he'd ridden right into town, anyway."

"Sure," Doc said, "reasonably safe, Henry."

He opened the door to leave, then looked back at Ives, who was slumped behind his desk.

"Don't be so hard on yourself, Henry."

"Sure, Doc," Ives said.

As Doc went out the door, he said, "Sure," again, but without much conviction.

NINETEEN

"Maybe the others took care of them," Ned Tyler said to Robak, who was looking behind them again.

"You really think so?" he asked.

"Why not?"

"They were all storekeepers, Ned," Robak said. "They had no chance against Clint Adams and that deputy."

"What if there's only one?" Tyler asked. "What if Adams came alone because the deputy couldn't ride."

"The deputy will ride."

"What if Adams didn't *want* to come after us?" Tyler asked. "What if he just left?"

"Clint Adams don't walk away, Ned," Robak said.

"How do you know?" Tyler asked. "You don't know him."

"I don't have to know him, Ned, I know about him," Robak said. "Don't you worry, they're both back there."

"So what do we do?" Tyler asked. "Wait for 'em? Ride harder? We'd need fresh horses if we're gonna ride—"

"We need some help."

"What kinda help?"

"Maybe," Ted Robak said, pointing ahead of them, "that kind."

Tyler looked ahead and saw a Conastoga wagon farther ahead of them.

"Who is that?"

"I don't know," Robak said. "Let's find out."

"Riders, Pa," ten-year-old Matthew Grady said.

"Joshua." Mary Grady grabbed her husband's arm and squeezed it tight.

"I see 'em, Mary," Joshua Grady said.

"You want your rifle, Pa?" the boy asked.

"Let's not assume anything, Matthew," Joshua said.

"Perhaps you should hold your rifle, Joshua."

"Hush, Mary," her husband said, "let's just see what they want."

Joshua Grady reined in his team and waited for the two riders to reach them.

"Good lookin' woman, Ted," Ned Tyler said.

"Forget the woman, Ned," Robak said. "Just keep quiet and let me do the talkin'."

"I'm just sayin'," Tyler said, "she's good lookin'."

"Shut up."

They rode up to the wagon, which had stopped to await them. There was a man and a woman sitting up top, and Robak thought he could see someone between them, in the back. And Robak had to agree that Tyler was right. The woman was good looking. She had yellow hair and pale skin and big blue eyes. She wasn't young, maybe in her thirties, but she *was* real good looking.

"Hello, there," Joshua Grady greeted them. "Is there something we can help you with?"

Robak could now clearly see a child in the back of the wagon.

"You know, friend," he said, "there just might be . . ."

Clint walked around the cold camp and said, "This is it. This is where they camped."

"How long ago?" Cole asked.

"A few hours, maybe less," Clint said, crouching over the cold fire. "We're getting closer."

"We got to catch up to them before they come in contact with some other people."

Clint looked at Cole.

"That's a good point, Jace," he said. "I've been thinking of keeping them away from other towns, but they could run across somebody on the trail."

"Then what do we do?" the deputy asked. "If they do come in contact with somebody else, we can't just let them go."

"No," Clint said, "we'd have to take them back to Safetown with us."

"What if they don't want to come?"

Clint stood up and brushed off his hands.

"Clint?"

"I'm afraid we wouldn't be able to give them that choice, Jace," Clint said, finally.

"You mean . . . we'd have to force them?"

"That's what I mean."

Jace Cole shook his head.

"That ain't exactly what I signed on for."

"None of this is, Jace," Clint said. "Come on, let's go."

TWENTY

"Don't hurt my wife or my boy," Joshua Grady said.

"We're not fixin' to hurt anybody, Mister," Robak said. "We just need to borrow them for a while."

Robak was sitting in Grady's place on the wagon, Grady's wife next to him and the boy still in the back, but tied up. The little monster had tried to strangle him.

Tyler was still astride his horse, holding the reins of Robak's horse in one hand and his gun in the other, trained on Joshua Grady. Grady was standing on the ground with a welt on his forehead. He, like the boy, had tried to stop Robak, who had clubbed the man with his gun. At that point the woman started shouting for them not to hurt her husband, she'd do whatever they wanted. That meant something entirely different to Ned Tyler than it did to Robak.

"I don't understand why you're doing this," Grady said. "We haven't done anything to you."

"You surely haven't, friend," Robak said.

"Then why?"

Robak shrugged.

"I'm afraid you were just in the wrong place at the wrong time," he said, finally.

"My family—"

"They'll be fine," Robak said, "as long as you and they do as you're told."

"What do you want me to do?"

"It's my guess," Robak said, "that within the next few hours two riders will approach from the south. When they do you tell them that we have your family."

"W-what if they don't care," Grady asked. "What if they won't want to help?"

"You don't want their help, Grady," Robak said. "We just want them to stop chasin' us, is all. You tell them that if they leave off chasin' us, we'll leave your family on foot a few miles from here."

"And our wagon?"

"We'll leave the wagon," Robak said, "but we'll scare off the horses."

Grady was going to argue about the horses, but then he figured he'd better take what he could get. At least he'd have his family back, and they'd have their belongings.

"All right," he said. "I'll tell them."

"There's a good man," Robak said.

"And what do you want of me and my son?" Mary Grady asked.

Robak looked at her.

"Ma'am," he said, "you just need to stay quiet and do what you're told to do."

"Must you leave him tied up like that?" she asked.

"We'll untie the boy after he calms down a little," Robak told him. He exchanged a glance with Tyler, who rolled his eyes and smiled. He was still thinking how the woman had said she'd do whatever they wanted her to do. He had some definite ideas about that.

"Are we all straight on what we have to do?" Robak asked. He was thinking about how good Mary Grady smelled, and how warm her hip felt pressed up against his. Then he realized he was thinking like Ned Tyler.

"I understand," Joshua Grady said. "But you have to understand something as well."

"What's that, Preacher?" Robak asked. He had no idea if Grady was a preacher or not, but he looked and dressed like one.

Grady ignored the remark.

"If you harm my family in any way," he said, "I will hunt you both down and kill you."

Robak stared at Grady and then said, "Okay, friend, we all understand each other."

"Aw, lemme put a bullet in 'im, Ted," Tyler said.

"No!" Mary Grady shouted.

"There's no reason to shoot the man, Ned," Robak said. "He and his family are just gonna help us out a little. Put your gun away."

Tyler obeyed, holstering his gun.

"If you do come lookin' for us, Grady," he couldn't resist saying, "we won't be the ones to die."

"We will see," Grady said, with more courage than he was feeling.

"Step back, Preacher," Robak said. "we don't want to run over your foot, now."

Grady took a few steps back.

"I love you, Mary," he said. "Take care of our boy."

"I love you, too, Joshua," she said. "I will. I promise."

"Sorry to break up such a touching scene," Robak

said, "but . . . hyah!!!" He snapped the reins and the
team of two horses took off running.

Joshua Grady took a few halting steps after them, but
then realized the futility behind it. He stopped and just
stood there watching the wagon, and his family, get farther and farther away.

"What are you wanted for?" Mary Grady asked, several
minutes later.

"Why do you want to know, Ma'am?"

"I would like to know if my son and I are in the hands
of killers, or just . . . miscreants."

"Well, Ma'am," he said, "since I don't have any idea
what a miscreant is, I'd have to go with the other one."

TWENTY-ONE

Clint was the first to see the man stumbling on foot toward them.

"Clint," Cole said.

"I see him."

The man was staggering, saw them, waved frantically, and then fell, as if the waving had taken the last of his energy.

"Let's go," Clint said, giving Eclipse a kick in the ribs. Cole followed.

When they reached the man, they dismounted and rushed to him. He seemed uninjured, except for a welt on his forehead. Other than that he simply seemed exhausted.

"Get your canteen," Clint said. Cole nodded, ran to his horse and returned with the water.

The man was trying to talk but did not have the energy. Clint supported him, keeping him in a seated position, and held the canteen to his lips. At first he pushed it away and continued to try to speak.

"You won't be able to speak until you've taken a drink," Clint told the man.

Finally, the exhausted man relented, accepted the drink and then had to be stopped from drinking too much too fast.

"All right," Clint said, taking the canteen away, "that's enough. Try to tell us what happened."

"Two . . ." the man said, then took a breath and tried again. "Two men . . . took my family . . . my wagon . . ."

"Okay," Clint said, "two men took your family and your wagon. Do you know who they were?"

"Were their names Robak and Tyler?" Jace Cole asked.

"Wha—no, not . . . not those . . ."

"First names," Clint said to Cole. "They'd be calling each other by their first names."

"Uh, oh, Ted and Ned," Cole said, then laughed because saying them out loud like that suddenly sounded funny.

"Yes . . . yes . . ." the man said. "They called each other . . . by those names . . ."

"Which way did they go?" Clint asked.

"Are you . . . are you the men pursuing them?" the man asked.

"Yes," Clint said, "we are. What's your name?"

"Grady," the man said. "Listen, you must stop . . . stop . . ."

"We intend to stop them, Mr. Grady," Clint said. "You have to tell us which way they went."

"No!" Grady said. He pushed himself away from Clint, accepted the responsibility for his own weight. "No, you mustn't go after them."

"Why not?" Cole asked.

"I told you," Grady said. "They have my family, my wife and my son."

"Why did they take them?"

"To keep you from going after them." Grady took a moment to look at Clint and Cole, saw the deputy's badge on the younger man's chest.

"You are the law?"

"I am."

"Are these men killers?"

Cole looked at Clint.

"They could be," Clint said.

Grady looked at Clint.

"You are not the law?"

"I'm just helping out."

Grady noticed that the younger man looked to Clint, so he directed his remarks to him.

"These men said they will not hurt my family," he said. "They said that if you left them alone they would leave my wife and my son by the side of the road, with our wagon. Did they lie about that?"

"Yes," Clint said, simply.

"I thought they might be lying," Grady said. "They told me to wait for you to come from the south, but I chose to start walking. I—I thought I would encounter you sooner."

"That was good thinking."

"Is there a chance . . . that they will not hurt my family?"

Clint looked to Cole for the answer, as he knew Tyler and Robak better than he did.

"There's always a chance," he said.

"Mr. Grady," Clint said, "we're sorry about your wife and son, and we will do everything in our power to get

them back unharmed, but we cannot stop pursuing these
two men. That simply isn't an option."

Grady thought for a moment, then said, "Then I will
come with you."

"No."

"Give me a gun," Grady said. "I can help."

Clint looked at the man critically, saw the same things
in him that Robak had seen.

"Are you a preacher of some kind, Mr. Grady?"

"No," the man said, "I'm a teacher, and a religious
man, but not a preacher. We come from the east. I'm on
my way to take up a post as a schoolteacher."

Clint hesitated a moment. What he would have preferred to do was leave the man a canteen and point him
toward the nearest town, but he had come into contact
with Robak and Tyler and there was no way to know if
they carried the disease or not.

"All right, Mr. Grady," he said, finally. "You can
come with us."

TWENTY-TWO

As much as he hated to put the extra added pressure on Eclipse, Clint allowed Grady to ride double with him. It would not have been a concern if he'd still been riding Duke. The big black gelding could have carried two men for miles and never felt it. However, this was the first such test for the Darley Arabian that had been a gift to him from P. T. Barnum.

When they reached the point where Robak and Tyler had taken Grady's family and wagon, Clint could see the tracks made by the Conestoga's wheels.

"Can't hide those," Cole said. "Even I can see them."

"What will we do?" Grady asked.

"We'll follow them," Clint said. "They'll be moving slower now that they have your wagon." He didn't add that they would also be moving slower because they were riding double. "We'll catch up to them eventually."

"Maybe," Grady said, "they'll keep their word and let them go, and we'll find them along the way."

Clint and Cole exchanged a glance that Grady couldn't see and Clint said, "Yeah, maybe."

87

• • •

Robak and Tyler did not come to a town before nightfall and finally decided to camp.

"If they keep riding they'll catch up," Tyler said.

"It don't matter," Robak said. "We got the woman and the boy as hostages. Even if they do catch up they can't do nothing."

They had untied the boy after going only a few miles, but soon after they did he had leaped from the back of the wagon and started running. Tyler had to ride him down and bring him back. After that they left him tied up in back of the wagon.

After Robak helped Mary Grady down from the wagon she asked, "Could we untie Matthew now?"

"I don't think so, lady," Robak said. "If he'd jump from a moving wagon then he's sure to run from camp. He stays tied up, and I want you to stay in the wagon with him."

"What about food?" she asked. "We're hungry."

"Don't worry," Robak said. "You'll get fed. Now, get in the wagon—and don't try untying him, or we'll tie you up, too."

Mary Grady climbed into the back of the wagon with her ten-year-old son, and it was the first time they had a chance to talk all day.

"Momma," he said, "you have to run."

"I can't run, sweetie," she said. "I can't leave you."

"Then untie me and I'll run," he said, "or we'll run together."

"We can't risk it, Matthew," she said. "Those men will hurt you."

"Then what do we do?"

"We just have to wait, and trust in God," she said. "Your father will come for us."

"Poppa?" the boy said. "He's a coward."

Mary recoiled and stared at her son in shock.

"Why would you ever say that about your father?"

"He let those men take us, Momma," the boy said. "He never shoulda done that."

"Your father did the best he could against men with guns, Matthew," she said.

"He shoulda taken the rifle when I offered it to him."

When Robak climbed up on the wagon, he had liberated the rifle, the only gun the Gradys owned.

"Matthew," she said, "I will not hear such talk about your father. He will come for us. You will see."

The boy cast his eyes downward and didn't say another word.

It was sometime later when Robak appeared at the back of the wagon.

"Lady? I got some food here for you and your boy."

"Thank you," she said. "We are very hungry."

She moved to the flap of the wagon and accepted the two plates filled with beans.

"May I untie him so he can eat?" she asked.

"I should make you feed him," Robak said, "but if you promise me he won't run, you can untie him."

"You have my word."

"Go ahead, then," Robak said, "but be warned, if he runs my partner will shoot him without hesitation."

"He will not run," she said, again.

"Then go ahead and eat."

As Robak walked away, she put the two plates of food down and untied her son.

"I can run now, Momma," the boy whispered. "We both can."

"We will do no such thing," she said. "You will eat, and keep up your strength so that when your father comes for us we will be ready."

"But Momma—"

"Hush, Matthew," she said, "and eat."

Robak returned to the fire and picked up his own plate.

"You really want me to shoot the kid?" Tyler asked, his mouth full of beans.

"Only if he runs."

"Can I have the woman?"

Robak thought a moment.

"She is real pretty, ain't she?" Robak asked.

"She sure is," Tyler said. "Prettier than any whore I ever been with. Can I have her?"

Robak didn't answer right away.

"We could both have her," Tyler said.

After a moment Robak said, "We'll see, Ned. We'll see."

TWENTY-THREE

"We have to stop," Jace Cole said.

"We can't stop," Grady insisted. "We have to catch up to them." During the course of the ride, Grady had decided that Robak and Tyler did actually plan to kill his wife and son. He was frantic to catch up to them. Clint knew that if they didn't reach them in time and they were killed, this man's guilt would consume him. He'd never forgive himself for not trying harder to prevent them from being taken—or die trying.

"Clint," Cole said, "my horse needs rest."

Clint could feel Eclipse's quivering beneath him, indicating that the Darley Arabian, too, needed rest. It was dark, and they hadn't yet caught up to Robak, Tyler and Grady's family, but they really had little choice at this point.

"All right," Clint said, finally. "Dismount. We'll camp for the night."

"But we can't—" Grady started, then stopped. "I'll go on by myself, on foot if I have to. Just give me a gun."

91

When they had all dismounted, Clint turned to face Grady.

"I'm not giving you a gun, Mr. Grady," he said. "You'll get your family and yourself killed."

"B-but . . . I must do something," the man insisted. "It's my fault they were taken, don't you see? I should have stopped them."

"Two men with guns?" Clint asked. "How do you think you could have stopped them?"

"I had a gun, too," Grady said, "a rifle in the back of the wagon. My son wanted to hand it to me, but I said no. I was wrong!"

"You were right," Clint said. "What kind of gun did you have?"

"A rifle."

"How well can you shoot?"

The man hesitated, then said, "Not well."

"You would have been killed the moment you tried to use it," Clint assured him. "Then you'd be dead and your family would have no chance at all. Now, at least, they have some."

"But if we wait until morning—"

"Mr. Grady, we have no choice," Clint said. "Our horses are ready to collapse. If we ride them into the ground then all of us will be in trouble, not just your family. Now settle down. We're going to make a fire and have some coffee and beef jerky. After that we'll all get some rest, and get an early start in the morning."

"I—I—" Grady started, then seemed to physically attempt to compose himself. "I think that you should call me Joshua, Mr. Adams, for the rest of our time together."

"All right, Joshua," Clint said. "I'm Clint and this is

Jace. Do you think you could collect some firewood?"

"Yes," Grady said, "yes, I can do that."

"Don't go too far, though."

"No," Grady said, "no, I won't."

Clint watched the man move off into the dark, wondering if he'd come back with firewood, or just keep going.

Joshua Grady considered just continuing to walk, but he knew that Clint Adams was right. Alone, he had no chance to get his family away from those two men. He had no choice but to stay with Adams and the deputy, and hope that they could save his wife and his son before they were killed.

When the fire was going they all sat around it and consumed their meager meal of coffee and beef jerky.

"May I ask a question?" Grady said, finally.

"Go ahead," Clint said. "We'll answer it if we can."

"Just exactly why are you after those men?"

Clint and Cole exchanged a glance, during which the deputy gave the question over to Clint.

"I guess you should know," Clint said.

"Know what?"

Clint took a deep breath and then told Joshua Grady about the disease that had infected Thanesville, causing the formation of a place called Safetown, from which Robak, Tyler and four other men had "escaped."

"And what happened to the other four men?" Grady asked.

"We caught up to them," Clint said.

"You . . . killed them?" Grady asked. "All four?"

"They didn't leave us much choice."

"I see."

Clint watched Grady, waiting for him to ask if his family was at risk of contracting the disease, but Joshua Grady had something else on his mind entirely.

He was thinking that if Clint and Jace Cole had killed four men already, then the chances of them killing the last two and saving his family were very good indeed.

TWENTY-FOUR

"Why do I have to take the first watch?" Ned Tyler complained.

"Because somebody has to do it," Robak said.

"Why don't you do it?"

"Because I'm taking the second watch."

Tyler frowned.

"Don't think about it, Ned," Robak said, "just do it."

"But I had plans—" Tyler said.

Robak got right in Tyler's face and said, "Forget about the woman. That's just not gonna happen."

"But you said yourself she's good lookin'."

"She is," Robak said. "Too good for you."

"Oh," Tyler said, "but not too good for you, huh?"

"Look," Robak said, "neither one of us is touchin' the woman, so just forget it. Wake me up at four . . . and stay alert. We don't want Adams and that deputy sneakin' up on us."

"Ain't nobody gonna sneak up on me," Tyler muttered to himself.

• • •

Robak walked over to the wagon before turning in.

"Do you need anything before I turn in?" he asked the woman. He ignored the child.

"No, thank you," Mary Grady said. "We're quite all right."

"If you need to do your business, now's the time," Robak said. "You can't be wakin' me up later."

"We're quite all right," Mary said. "We don't need to . . . to do our business."

Robak stared at Mary Grady long enough for her to grow uncomfortable beneath his gaze.

"You think I'm pretty crude, don't ya?" he asked, finally.

"At the risk of making you angry," she said, "yes."

"I ain't mad," Robak said. "I know I'm crude, so it don't make me mad to have you think of me that way."

"Then why did you ask?"

"Just curious," Robak said. "You know, it would do you some good to be nice to me."

"What kind of good would that do?"

"Well, my partner," Robak said, "he's been sort of thinkin' about you in a crude way, if you get my meaning."

"Neither one of you better touch my mother!" the boy snapped, angrily. Apparently, he also understood what Robak meant.

"Shut up, boy," Robak said. "You shouldn't interrupt when adults are talkin'."

"You just better not touch her, that's all," Matthew said.

"You should teach your whelp some manners," Robak said.

"My son," Mary Grady said, encircling the boy in her

arms protectively, "has impeccable manners, which is
something I cannot say for you . . ."

"Robak," he said. "My name's Robak, Ted Robak."

"Mr. Robak," Mary said, "I believe it is time for all
of us to get some sleep. If I am any judge, we have a
long day ahead of us tomorrow."

"Oh yeah, we do," Robak said, "but then, some of us
might have a long night ahead of us, too."

With that ominous statement hanging in the air, he
disappeared from the back of the wagon.

"What's gonna happen, Momma?" the boy asked,
now more frightened than angry.

"Nothing's going to happen, Matthew," she said. "I
told you. Your father will find us."

"I get the feeling," the boy said, "that if he's gonna
find us, it better be soon."

Mary Grady didn't say it out loud, but she had the
same feeling her son did.

Robak was angry with himself. He wanted the woman,
and that made him mad, because it made him no better
than Tyler. Oh, there were some differences. Tyler
would have simply raped the woman if Robak would let
him. Robak, however, was a lot of things, but a rapist
was not one of them. He actually had more respect for
women than that, which was something that probably
would have surprised a lot of people.

He went to his bedroll and rolled himself up in it. He
had placed himself halfway between the fire and the
wagon. He was pretty sure that even though he was on
watch, Tyler would try for the woman during the night.
Robak wanted to be in a position to stop him.

In fact, Robak would not have minded killing Tyler

and leaving him behind—him and the boy. He and the woman could make a lot better time without them. He wouldn't kill the boy, though. Just leave him by the side of the road. Maybe the father would be satisfied with getting the boy back and wouldn't come after the woman.

He drew his gun from his holster, intending to go to sleep with it in his hand. Ned Tyler didn't know it, but he was real close to having his last night on this earth.

TWENTY-FIVE

Doc Beacham hated waking up in the morning. Sometimes he felt as if the best thing for him would be to just die in his sleep. But it didn't happen. He woke each morning and he knew he had to go out, make his rounds, find out how many more had died during the night.

Up to this point, Matt Foley had been the only one of the seven to die. He knew that if any of the others died he was going to have to send a telegram to the state capital for assistance—but until that happened, it was all up to him. If only, by some miracle, the dying would stop . . .

Jenny Thane awoke and remained on her cot, lying on her back, staring at the top of the tent. Another day of waiting. So far the people of Safetown had been just that, safe. She was dreading, however, the time when some of them would begin to exhibit the symptoms of the disease. When that happened there would be no safe place for any of them to go. Only those with some unknown immunity to the disease would survive, and they would have to rebuild.

She thought about Clint Adams, out there chasing Ted Robak and his cronies. If any of them should reach another town, or a densely populated city . . . It was too horrible to think about.

Jenny pushed herself to a seated position, then pushed again to get herself to stand. Time to make her rounds and then go to see Doc Beacham. Maybe what Clint had said about the animals would help . . .

Mary Grady awoke and looked down at her son, Matthew, who had fallen asleep with his head in her lap. She kept telling the boy that his father would come for them, but did she really believe it? Joshua had been on foot with no food, no water, and no weapons. How could he possibly save them? She was going to have to figure out a way to save them herself or, at least, to save her son.

Clint Adams had taken the last watch, so he was up and around to watch the sunrise. He put on a fresh pot of coffee, but they had no beef jerky left. The coffee would have to do. He looked over at Jace Cole and Joshua Grady, still wrapped in their blankets, asleep. Grady was using Clint's blanket since he had nothing of his own. Everything he owned or had in the world was out there with Ted Robak, and God only knew what he was going to do with it all. He'd probably discard the wagon and its contents at some point but keep the woman and the boy as hostages. Or maybe he'd leave one of them behind, too. Why would he need more than one hostage? If that was the case, which one would he keep? Were he and his partner the kind of men who would keep the woman and hard use her? What would poor Joshua Grady think if he got his wife back, beaten and raped?

Clint poured himself another pot of coffee. Now not only did he have to make sure that Robak and Tyler didn't reach another town, but he had to try to do it without getting the Grady woman and boy killed.

He wondered how things were going back in Thanesville and in Safetown. Jenny would be seeing the Doc again, today. Would she tell him what Clint had said about the animals? And would that be any help at all? And what of Henry Ives? What was his condition? And how was he feeling, since a badge was little help against what was plaguing his town, right now.

If Clint knew Henry Ives at all, the man was feeling lost, and useless . . .

Ted Robak poured himself another cup of coffee. He'd taken the last watch, and he'd gotten through the night without having to kill Ned Tyler. In a little while he'd wake the woman and have her make breakfast. After all, the wagon was filled with supplies, and he and Ned hadn't had a decent meal in a while. The beans they'd eaten last night had been good, but there was flour in the wagon and he had an urge for some flapjacks this morning.

And why not take their time and have a good breakfast? Even if Adams and the deputy—and the husband—caught up to them, what could they do as long as Robak and Tyler were holding the woman and the boy?

Robak put the cup of coffee down and wiped his forehead with his sleeve. It wasn't that hot a morning, so
why was he sweating? There was nothing to sweat
about. He and Tyler were in charge of their own desti-
nies now—and he was in charge of Ned Tyler's.

He got up and went to wake the woman.

Henry Ives woke and slipped out of bed without waking Hannah. He walked to the window and looked
down. This seemed to be all he could do these days.
Why, he wondered, should he even put his badge on
this morning? What good was it to anyone? What good
was he?

He then saw Doc Beacham on the street, making his
early rounds, checking to see if anyone had died during the night—and suddenly it hit him. This whole situation had to be even harder on Doc than it was on
him. It was Doc who was charged with keeping the
people of Thanesville healthy, and here they were dying all around him. Why was Henry Ives feeling so
depressed, so useless, when it was Doc who was suffering the most?

Poor Doc, he thought. He still goes out there on the
street with his medical bag, his "badge," no matter what
happens.

Ives turned away from the window and picked his
shirt up off the chair he'd draped it over. The badge
was still pinned to it. He held it so that the light from
the window reflected off the star. He'd continue to
wear the badge as long as Doc continued to go out
carrying his medical bag. If Doc could face this epidemic each day, then how could Sheriff Henry Ives do

any less? The people of this town were looking to the two of them for help, and neither of them could afford to give up.

None of them could.

TWENTY-SIX

"Do you think we'll catch up to them today?" Joshua Grady asked as they were breaking camp.

The answer to that question was, "Yes, if we could leave you behind and not have to ride double." But Clint didn't say that. What he said instead was, "Probably."

"We have to," Cole said. "We can't let them reach another town."

"Because of this disease they are carrying?" Grady asked.

"May be carrying," Clint said. "Mr. Grady, if we do have to go into a town, it's important we don't start a panic until we know if there's something to start a panic over."

"I don't want to start anything," Grady said. "I just want to get my family back."

"I understand that," Clint said. "We're all working toward the same end here. Let's get mounted."

He climbed aboard Eclipse, then reached down to help Grady up behind him. So far the black Darley had done

everything he'd asked of him, but he hoped this would
be the last day of riding double.

Mary Grady dished out the flapjacks for Robak and Tyler, then asked, "May I bring some to my son?"

"Less for us that way," Tyler observed.

"Go ahead, Ma'am," Robak said, ignoring Tyler.
"And take some for yourself."

She did so, filling two plates and then walking back
to the wagon with them.

"You're getting soft on her," Tyler said.

"What?"

"That's why you won't let me have her."

Robak glared at Tyler.

"Ned," he said, "we might be coming to the point in
our partnership when it's time to split up."

"Oh, yeah," Tyler said, "I go one way and you and
the woman go another. Then what do I do for a hostage?"

"You take the boy."

"The boy?"

"We cut the team loose and leave the wagon behind.
You put the boy on one horse, I'll put the woman on
the other, and we go our separate ways."

"And what about the supplies?"

"We split 'em."

Tyler stuffed his mouth with flapjacks and thought it
over. Let Robak have the woman if he wanted her. As
soon as he got to the nearest town he could get himself
a whore that was better than her.

"Okay," Tyler said, "fine. We'll split up. I'll keep the
boy with me until I reach a town, and then . . . I'll cut
his throat."

"You do what you want with him," Robak said.

"And how long are you gonna keep the woman?"

"Until I don't need her anymore," Robak said. "Unlike you, I'm not in a hurry to kill anybody."

"I ain't in no hurry to kill nobody," Tyler said. "I just don't need to have no kid with me for long."

"Fine."

Tyler poured himself another cup of coffee and used it to wash down the last of the flapjacks.

"You better not keep the woman too long, Robak."

"Why's that?"

"That husband of hers is gonna want her back," Tyler said. "He'll keep comin' after her."

"And he won't come after you for the boy?"

"Who would you want back more?" Tyler asked. "Your woman, or some boy?"

"That's his son, Tyler."

"Same thing. He's gonna want his woman."

Robak stuffed the last of his flapjacks into his mouth and said, "I'll keep that in mind."

Mary Grady climbed into the back of the wagon and untied her son's hands. He eagerly accepted the plate of flapjacks and started eating. She, on the other hand, nibbled.

"What's the matter, Momma?" he asked. "Ain't you hungry?"

"I'm thinking, Matthew."

"About what?"

"About what you said."

"What'd I say?"

"That we should run."

"I'm ready to run, Momma," he said, eagerly.

"We're not going to do anything until I say so, all right, Matthew?"

"All right, Momma," he said. "I'll run when you say—but when will that be?"

"Soon," she said, "I think very soon."

TWENTY-SEVEN

"What are you doing?" Mary Grady demanded.

"I'm unhitching the team," Robak said. "We won't be needing the wagon anymore."

"B-but, all of our belongings are in the wagon."

"You can come back for them," he said. "Or your husband might come along and pick them up."

"B-but . . . what are we going to do about the horses?"

"Don't worry," Robak said, "we're keeping the horses with us. You and your boy are going to ride."

"Bareback?"

"Is that a problem?"

"Yes," she said. "Neither of us rides very well."

"You'll just have to try," Robak said. "I don't know about Tyler and your boy, but I'm not going to want you to slow me down."

"Wait a minute," she said. "What did you mean, Tyler and my boy? You don't mean—"

Robak turned on her and snapped, "Tyler and I are splitting up. He's takin' the boy, I'm takin' you. It's as simple as that."

"You—you can't do that!" she exclaimed. "I can't leave my son."

"You ain't got a choice."

"I most certainly do—" She was cut off when he slapped her, a stinging blow that made her eyes water. She had never been struck before.

"You'll do what you're told, woman!" he snapped. "And so will your whelp, if he knows what's good for him."

"You can't separate us," she cried. "You can't."

"Don't you hit my mom!" the boy's voice came from inside the wagon.

"You better go and tell your boy to shut up," Robak said, "or I might just decide to leave him by the side of the road—dead."

"You wouldn't kill a little boy," she said, aghast. "You couldn't be that much of a monster."

"Don't try me, lady," Robak said.

She stared at him a few more moments in disbelief, then hurried to the back of the wagon to talk to Matthew. She had waited too long to make a decision in whether to run or not. If they tried it now and failed, she was sure the two men would kill her and her son.

"Matthew," she said, climbing into the back of the wagon, "You have to listen to me very carefully."

Sheriff Henry Ives looked up as Doc Beacham entered his office. Without a word the older man walked to the potbellied stove in the corner and poured himself a mug of coffee, then carried it to the desk and sat down heavily in a chair directly opposite the lawman.

"How many?" Ives asked. "How many died during the night?"

"Three," Beacham replied, wearily.

"How many children?"

Beacham stared at Ives and said, "All three."

"God help them," Ives said.

"God help us, Henry," Beacham said.

Ives sat forward.

"Doc, you got to send for help."

"What can anyone do?"

"Somebody might know what this is," Ives said. "Somebody might know what to do to stop it."

"You know what the mayor said, Henry—"

"I don't care what you and your council members are afraid of, Doc," Ives said. "Something's got to be done."

Beacham had taken only one sip of coffee and now put the mug on the desk. He stood up and stared down at it.

"I'll think about it, Henry," he said. "I have to go."

"Doc—"

"It's my decision, Henry," Beacham said. "Don't try making it for me."

Beacham left and Ives sat back in his chair. Could he afford *not* to make the decision?

Doc Beacham decided to talk things over with Jenny Thane before he made his final decision about sending for help. The problem with sending for help now was that the authorities would want to know why he waited so long in the first place.

What could he tell them?

Mary Grady watched as Robak lifted her son onto the back of the horse. The boy's hands were tied in front of him, but he was not tied to the horse, and his feet were not tied. His mother's instructions were to take the first opportunity he could to try to escape.

"I can't go without you, Momma," the boy said, bravely holding back tears.

"If you get away, Matthew, you can find your father and come back for me," she said. She had smoothed his hair down and cupped his face in her hands. "You have to do it."

As she watched Tyler ride away with her son, who was craning his neck to look back at her, she knew the boy had only one chance to live, and that was to get away.

It was her only chance as well.

TWENTY-EIGHT

Robak tied Mary Grady's hands together and then lifted her up onto the other team horse.

"If you try to get away," he said to her, "I'll have to hurt you."

"If my son is hurt, or . . ." her voice caught, ". . . or killed, I swear I will see you dead."

"Yeah," he said, "you and your husband and lots of other people would like to see me dead."

He wiped his head with his sleeve, wondering why he was so hot.

"You look like you have a fever."

"What?"

"Your eyes look feverish," she said, "and you're sweating. Why are you sweating so much?"

He frowned at her.

"I ain't got a fever!" he said, quickly. "Don't even say that."

Wasn't that what happened to the ones who died, he asked himself? Didn't they get a fever first?

He went around to his own horse and mounted up. As

he swung into the saddle he suddenly became a little light-headed.

Mary Grady, who had nursed many people back to health, knew a sick person when she saw one, and Robak was sick. This, then, was probably the chance she had been waiting for.

"Let's go," he said, "and don't fall off your horse!"

"I—I'll try not to."

All she had to do was watch and wait for a weak moment, a perfect moment for her to make her move. Whatever ailment he had, it was probably just beginning, and it would get worse before it got better. If she was lucky he'd faint and fall off *his* horse, but in truth she probably only had to wait for a weak moment so she could try to escape.

Of course, having him drop dead was probably too much to ask, and even wishing it would have been a sin.

"That's my wagon!" Grady shouted. "That's our wagon." He tried to get Eclipse to go faster but could not do that from his position behind Clint.

"Take it easy, Mr. Grady," Clint said. "This could be a trap."

"My wife and son could be in that wagon," he said, desperately.

"If they are," Clint said, "they're not going anywhere. Let's just make sure this is not a trap before we go riding in there."

"What kind of trap?" Grady asked. He looked around at the flatlands around them. "Where could anyone hide?"

Clint looked at Grady and said, "In the wagon."

Grady realized how right Clint was and both felt and looked silly.

"Oh."

"Just slide down to the ground and stay there," Clint said. "Jace, say here with him."

"Okay."

Clint rode forward slowly, ready to draw his gun at a moment's notice. As he drew closer his instincts told him there was no trap. No one was inside the wagon. It had simply been abandoned. When he reached it he dismounted, approached the wagon and looked inside. Satisfied that he was right, he turned and waved for Grady and Cole to join him.

"What did you find?" Grady asked anxiously when he reached the wagon.

"Nothing," Clint said. "Look for yourself."

Grady looked inside the wagon, then climbed in to have a better look.

"Did they take anything?" Cole asked.

"Some supplies," Grady said, "b-but, where's my family?"

"Over here," Clint said.

Cole and Grady joined him.

"They split up," Clint said, pointing to the ground. "They put your wife and son on one of the team horses and split up."

"You mean . . . they separated my wife and my boy?"

"That's right."

"But . . . why?"

"My guess is to split us up," Clint said. "Robak took one that way"—he pointed north—"and Tyler took one that way," and pointed west.

"But . . . which one do we follow?"

Clint had been crouched over the tracks as he examined them, and now he straightened up.

"We'll have to do what they want us to do," he said. "Split up. Jace, you ride west, and I'll follow the tracks north."

"All right, Clint."

"B-but what do I do?" Grady asked. "Which tracks do I follow? Which are my wife's and which are my son's?"

"Does it matter, Mr. Grady?" Clint asked.

He could see the man wrestling with the answer.

"Well . . . no, I suppose not . . ."

"Then why don't you go with Jace," Clint said. "You can ride double with him."

Cole looked as if he wanted to complain, but Clint had been riding double with Grady since yesterday. He supposed it was his turn.

"All right," he said.

"Jace, let's get in the wagon and take some supplies," Clint said.

"Do you really think we'll need—" Cole started, but Clint cut him off.

"Let's take a look, Jace," he said, firmly.

"All right, Clint."

Cole dismounted and climbed into the back of the wagon with Clint, who peered out the back to see what Grady was doing. The man was staring at the tracks in the ground, as if they could tell him something.

"What's going on, Clint?" Cole asked. "We don't need to outfit ourselves, we've got to catch them today."

"I know," Clint said. "I want you to take Mr. Grady because I'll be tracking Robak and his wife."

"How do you know that your tracks belong to Robak and Mrs. Grady?" Cole asked.

"I can make out the tracks of two men, a woman and a boy," Clint said. "I know that the tracks I'm following belong to the woman. I also figure that Robak would take the woman, don't you?"

"Well . . . yeah. I mean, it'd probably be his choice, Tyler wouldn't go against him."

"I don't want Grady with me when I find his wife," Clint said. "Just in case . . ."

"Just in case what . . . oh."

"It's better that he finds the boy with you," Clint said. "Can you handle Tyler?"

"I guess I'm gonna have to find out," Cole said, "ain't I?"

"I'm afraid so, Jace," Clint replied.

TWENTY-NINE

Jenny reached the clearing first and had to wait twenty minutes for Doc to arrive.

"Where's Mr. Adams?"

"We had some trouble," she said, and told him about Robak and his men leaving Safetown.

"My God," he said, "if they reach another town . . ."

"Both Clint and Jace are after them, Doc," Jenny said. "How about things in town?"

"We lost three overnight," he said. "All children."

"Oh, God." She covered her face with her hands, then dropped them down. "What are we going to do, Doc?"

"I don't know," he said. "I've been thinking about sending for help."

"Will you check with Uncle Horace first?"

"If I do that he will tell me not to do it," Doc Beacham said. "I don't know what to do, Jenny."

"Doc," she said, "Clint asked me something, and I want to ask you."

"Go ahead."

"Have any animals been affected by the disease?"

119

"Animals?"

"Horses, dogs—"

"I know what animals are, damn it!" he snapped.

"I'm sorry, Doc . . . I didn't mean . . ."

"No, I'm sorry, Jenny," Doc said. "Please forgive me. Now that you mention it there have been no cases of dogs or horses dying."

"That was what I thought."

Doc seemed deep in thought for a moment, then appeared to become excited.

"No, that's right," he said, "no animals have been affected. Why didn't I see this before?"

"I think we're too close to it, Doc," she said. "I think it took someone like Clint to walk in and look at the situation with fresh eyes."

"That's got to mean something, Jenny," Doc Beachan said. "It's got to."

"I hope so, Doc."

"I'm going to go back to town and give this some more thought."

"How is Sheriff Ives?" she asked. "Clint will want to know when he comes back."

"Henry's fine, Jenny," Doc said. "Just fine. No symptoms."

"And Hannah?"

"The same."

"That's about the only good thing that's happened in all this time," Jenny said. "The two of them finding each other."

"It's taken them long enough," Doc said. "We all knew they belonged together long before they did. Dear, I have to get back. I want to work on this new development right away."

"All right, Doc. Two more days?"

"One," he said. "Let's meet every day now. Same time tomorrow."

"All right, Doc," she said. "I'll see you tomorrow."

"Animals," she heard him mutter as he climbed onto his buckboard. "Imagine that."

Mary Grady tried twice to get away, but both times Robak was too fast for her. First, even though her hands were tied together in front of her, she tried to grab his gun from his holster. She did manage to get her hands on it, but he kept her from going any further. The next time she tried sliding off the back of the horse so she could run, but when she hit the ground she ended up knocking the wind out of herself. Of course, she would have had a better chance of escaping if she'd been riding her own horse, but soon after they had split up from Tyler and her son, the horse she was riding stepped into a chuckhole and went lame. Robak had not bothered to shoot the animal, but had simply left it behind while they rode double. He enjoyed having her body pressed against the back of him, especially her full breasts.

He stood over her and said, "You're gonna end up hurting yourself if you keep trying to get away."

"Why don't you let me go?" she asked.

"I kinda like you," he said.

"I thought you wanted me as a hostage?"

He reached down and hauled her to her feet. Her disheveled appearance and the smell of her sweat aroused him. He was well past the point where he was trying to convince himself he *didn't* want her. At least he was different from Tyler in that he didn't want to just rape her.

"I did," he said, "at first, but I'm afraid that now I just . . . well, I just want you."

She stared at him for a few moments, then realized what he was talking about.

"Oh, no," she said, "no, I could never—"

"Never what?" he demanded. "Want someone like me?"

"I could never want *any* man," she said. "I'm married, and I love my husband."

"That coward?"

"He's not a coward."

"He didn't try very hard to keep me from taking you, did he?" Robak sneered.

"You had guns."

"He had a gun."

"He's not a violent man."

"Any man fights for his woman," Robak said.

"You don't understand," she said. "He's a kind, gentle man. He'd never allow—"

"And he allowed you to be taken from him."

"He would never—"

"It don't matter," he said, cutting her off. "Come on, you're gonna ride in front of me from now on." The thought of having her pressed against the front of him aroused him even more.

"Mr. Robak, please—"

Suddenly, Robak seem to stagger and sway and his vision became fuzzy.

"Mr. Robak?"

He squinted, but was only able to faintly make out her shape. It was as if the sun were suddenly shining directly into his eyes.

"Mr. Robak, are you all right?"

He closed his eyes, rubbed them, then ran his sleeve over his brow to wipe away the sweat. When he opened his eyes his vision had returned to normal.

"You're not well," she said.

"Shut up!" he said. "I'm fine."

This couldn't be the disease. It couldn't! It must just be the result of all the riding they'd been doing and not eating right. Yeah, that was it. As soon as he had some rest and some real food he'd be good as new.

"Let's go, lady," he said. "Up on the horse."

"But, Mr. Robak—"

"Now!"

THIRTY

"I see something," Jace Cole said.

"What?" Joshua Grady asked.

"Up ahead," Cole said. "I think I see two riders."

Grady had to lean over to see past Cole's body.

"I see them, too."

"Now the question is," Cole said, "will they see us before we can reach them?"

"How can we avoid it?" Grady asked.

"Well," Cole said, "we can drop back and circle around to try to intercept them."

Grady squinted.

"Can you see if he has my wife or my son with him?"

"No," Cole said, "I can't make that out."

He reined in his horse, then turned and headed north.

"What are you doing?"

"We're going to circle around to the north and try to get in front of him," Cole said.

"What if he changes direction?"

"Then we'll find him again," Cole said. "He's within eyesight now, Mr. Grady. We won't lose him."

"Well, all right," Grady said. "This is your business. I suppose you know what you're doing."

Not really, Cole thought, but he knew more than he did before he started riding with Clint.

Clint reined in and stood up in his stirrups. It was a pleasure to once again have his saddle to himself. What he saw was a horse without a saddle, apparently hobbling on an injured leg. He sat back down in the saddle and rode toward the horse. That the animal did not shy away from him meant it wasn't wild. When he got close enough to examine it he saw the markings on it from having been hooked up to a wagon on and off for a long time. Not a saddle animal.

He dismounted and approached the horse, speaking to it to soothe it. It wasn't necessary, though. The horse was very docile and did not mind when he lifted it's legs to examine them. Sure enough, it had an injury to the right foreleg. It had probably stepped into a hole of some kind and wrenched. The injury appeared to be one that would heal with time, so there was no need to destroy the animal. Robak must have simply decided to set it free and ride double with Mrs. Grady. Now it was Robak who was carrying the extra weight in his saddle. That should make it easier to catch up to them now.

He remounted and continued to follow tracks that were now of a single horse.

"It's the boy," Cole said.

"I can see that," Grady said. The man did not sound happy that they had found his son, not his wife. Cole also silently marvelled at the fact that Clint had been right about which man had taken which hostage.

They had circled around and now the two riders were approaching them. From a sign they had encountered, Cole knew that the nearest town was now two miles away. He could not allow Cole to get by him.

He had ordered Grady to dismount and hold on to the horse's reins. He picked a stand of three that were dense enough to hide the horse and the man and told Grady to stay behind them.

"But why?"

"I've got to convince Tyler when he tries to use your boy as a hostage that I don't care," Cole said. "If he sees you, and knows that the boy's father is here with me, he won't believe that."

"But . . . you do care."

"But I can't let Tyler know that," Cole said. "Look, Grady, just do as I say and we'll get your boy back, all right?"

Glumly, Grady agreed.

"Once we do," Cole added, "you can ask him about your wife."

Grady brightened and said, "That's right."

"Okay," Cole said, "they're coming. Get behind those trees and stay there."

Grady obeyed, and Cole stepped out to face Tyler, his heart feeling as if it were in his throat.

Clint spotted the two people riding double and slowed his pace. He didn't want Robak to realize he was there. He also realized that he should have warned Cole about that, also. Maybe the deputy had learned enough during their short time together to realize on his own that he would not be able to simply ride up on Tyler without giving himself away.

Clint couldn't worry about that now, though. Tyler was the deputy's problem, and Ted Robak was his.

He turned Eclipse east and began to circle around to get in front of Robak and Mrs. Grady.

THIRTY-ONE

When Tyler saw Jace Cole, he couldn't believe it. Hurriedly, he reached over and grabbed the reins of the horse Matthew Grady was riding. Matthew's hands were tied in front of him, and he had been waiting for a chance to try to escape.

"Just keep your mouth shut, boy." These were the first words Tyler had spoken to Matthew since they had started riding.

Matthew looked ahead, saw the man standing there and saw the sun glint off of something metallic on his chest.

A badge.

"Hold it right there, Tyler," Jace Cole said.

"Well, well," Tyler said. "You came a long way to die, Deputy."

"We have to go back, Tyler," Cole said. "You know why."

"You think you can take me back, Jace?"

"You don't have Robak and the others to back you

up, Ned," Cole said. "Yeah, I think I can take you back."

"What happened to the others, by the way?" Tyler asked.

"They're dead."

"You and Adams?"

"That's right."

"Well," Tyler said, shifting his weight in the saddle, "You ain't got Adams to back you up, do you, Jace?"

"Don't need him, Ned," Cole said. "This is just me and you."

"Me, you . . . and the boy," Tyler said. "Don't forget I got me the boy, Deputy."

"He hurt you, Matthew?"

"No, sir," the boy said. "He hasn't spoken to me, but he hasn't hurt me. How do you know my name?"

"Your father told me."

"You've seen my father?"

"Yes, I have."

"Is he coming to get me?" Matthew asked. "Is he?"

Joshua Grady could not keep silent a moment longer.

"I'm here, Matthew," he said, stepping out from hiding. "I'm here to get you."

"Poppa!"

"I'll kill the boy, Jace!" Tyler said. "You know I will."

Cole saw two things happening at once. As Ned Tyler went for his gun Matthew threw himself off his horse. With the boy falling away from Tyler, away from danger, Cole felt free to draw his gun.

He only hoped he could draw it in time.

As Jace Cole had done, Clint also circled around so that Ted Robak and Mary Grady were now riding toward him. Unlike Cole's situation, however, Robak had the woman riding double with him, and in front of him. Clint was going to have to be very careful how he played this.

He had left Eclipse far enough away so that any noise he might make would not alert Robak to his presence. Clint had found a collection of rocks in Robak's path and hoped that Robak would not choose to ride around them rather than go right through them. There was certainly enough room for him to ride between them. Clint chose the largest one and hid himself behind him.

He had the feeling that he was going to have to do this without his gun. He just hoped that Ted Robak would cooperate.

THIRTY-TWO

For a while, Robak enjoyed the feel of Mary Grady leaning back against him. He even brushed her breasts a time or two with his arms while holding the reins. But for the past hour he'd been feeling pretty sick. He was hot, sweating more than ever, his eyes were blurry and he felt as if his throat were so swollen he'd never be able to swallow again.

"Goddamnit," he said, under his breath—but still loud enough for Mary Grady to have heard.

"What's wrong?"

They were approaching an outcropping of rocks, and she thought that maybe he'd seen something.

"Nothing," he said.

"Is something—"

"Just forget it."

"Are we going to ride into those rocks?" she asked.

"Don't worry about it," he said. He couldn't see any rocks, so he just let his horse have his lead. If the animal wanted to walk into some rocks, what the hell was the difference?

Ted Robak knew that he had the disease. If he'd stayed behind in Safetown maybe they could have done something for him, but on the other hand, probably not. He'd probably be in the same situation then that he found himself in right now.

He was going to die.

As the double-mounted horse came through the rocks, Clint did the only thing he thought he could do. He leaped from behind the rocks and grabbed Robak, pulling him from the saddle. He knew there was a good chance the woman would be pulled down as well, but since he couldn't use his gun, this was his best chance.

The man and the woman tumbled from the saddle and Clint abruptly changed his plan. Rather than grab Robak again, he instead grabbed the woman and pulled her to safety behind some rocks.

"Are you all right?" he asked her.

"I'm fine," she said, "but he's not."

"What?"

"Something's wrong with him," she said. "I—I don't think he can see."

Clint remembered that the man he'd found in the mass grave had been blind.

"He's so hot, and sweating, and he mutters to himself, and I—I think he's blind."

Clint looked down at his hands, realizing he had just touched Robak.

"Damn!" he said.

"Wow!" Matthew Grady said, getting to his feet.

His father rushed to him and put his arms around him, but Matthew was staring at Jace Cole.

"You shot him right out of the saddle!" he exclaimed.

Cole, who was still holding his gun out, said, "Yeah, I guess I did."

"Wow," Matthew said, again.

"Are you okay, son?" Grady asked, holding his son at arm's length and examining him for damage.

"I'm all right, Poppa," he said, "but I'm sorry."

"About what?"

"I—I told Momma you were a coward, but she said you weren't," Matthew explained. "She said you'd come for us, and you have. I—I'm sorry."

"That's all right, son," Grady said, hugging the boy, "it's all right."

Cole walked over to check on Ned Tyler to make sure he was dead, then walked back to the boy and his father.

"Matthew, we have to ask you something," he said.

"What?"

"Was this man complaining about feeling sick?"

"No."

"What about the other man?"

"He wasn't complaining, either," Matthew said, but then he added, "but he looked sick."

"What do you mean he looked sick?" Cole asked.

"Well, he was sweating all the time, even when it wasn't hot," Matthew said. He looked at his father. "Doesn't that mean you're sick?"

"Sometimes it does, yes," Joshua Grady said.

"That other man has Momma," Matthew said. "Are we going to go get her?"

"There is already a man doing that, Matthew," Cole said, "but we're all gonna go and meet them. Mr. Grady?"

"Yes?"

"You can have Tyler's horse."

"A dead man's horse?"

"Would you rather walk?"

"I'll take his horse," Grady said. "What about you, Matthew? Want to ride with me?"

"I can ride this one, Poppa," the boy said. "I'm getting pretty good at riding without a saddle. Isn't that how the Indians ride, Mister?"

"I'm Deputy Cole, Matthew," Cole said, "and yes, that's how the Indians ride."

THIRTY-THREE

"Robak?" Clint called from behind the rocks.

"Adams?" Robak yelled out. "Is that you?"

"It's me."

"You gotta help me."

"Why?"

"I'm sick," Robak said. "I don't wanna die like the others."

"If you're sick, Robak," Clint said, looking down at his hands, "there's nothing I can do for you."

"Yeah, there is."

"What's that?"

"Finish me," Robak said. "Don't let me die the way the others did."

"What's he talking about?" Mary Grady asked.

"I'll explain later."

"Does—does he have some sort of disease?" she asked, her hand going to her throat. "He's touched me, and my son."

"And me," Clint said, "and there's no guarantee that any of us will catch what he has."

"But . . . is there a guarantee we won't?"

"No."

"Mr. . . . Adams, did he say?"

"My name is Clint Adams, Ma'am," Clint said, "but I'll have to ask you to be quiet now."

"But the other man, he has my son—"

"A deputy has gone after him, with your husband along, Ma'am," Clint assured her.

"My husb—"

"Ma'am, please!"

She fell silent.

"Robak?" Clint asked. "Is this some kind of a trick?"

"No trick, Adams," Robak said. "Jesus, man, I can't see!"

Clint stepped out from behind the rocks and saw Robak on his knees. He was holding his hands out in front of him, but he couldn't see them. It was obvious he wasn't faking, the poor bastard.

But this poor bastard wasn't worried about infecting others, was he?

"Why should I help you, Robak?" Clint asked. "You could have stayed in Safetown, but you chose to ride all over the country. Maybe spreading this disease around."

"I—I didn't think I'd get it."

"What about this woman, and her son? What about them?"

"I—I'm sorry . . . Ma'am? Are you there?"

Clint turned and looked at Mary, who had also stepped our from the rocks. He nodded for her to answer.

"I—I'm here, Mr. Robak."

"Ma'am, I'm truly sorry about this," Robak said. "I—I didn't think—"

"No, Mr. Robak," she said, "obviously you didn't."

"This don't mean you'll get it, Ma'am," Robak said. "There's still lots of folks who ain't got it."

"I see," Mary said.

"Ya gotta forgive me, Ma'am," Robak said, "I'm askin' ya."

She closed her eyes and said, "Yes, all right, Mr. Robak. I forgive you."

"Thank you, Ma'am," Robak said. "Adams? Finish me off, Adams. You did it for Matt Foley."

"Robak, Foley was in bad shape—"

"And I'm gonna get there," Robak said. "I know I am. Adams?"

"Yes?"

"I ain't got the guts to do it myself," Robak said. "I— I just ain't got the guts. You gotta do it for me."

"Yes," Clint said, drawing his gun, "I suppose I do."

As they rode back to find Cole and Grady and—hope-fully—the boy, Clint told Mary Grady about Thanesville and Safetown.

"So I suppose you'll have to take us back to Safetown with you," she said, when he finished. "To make sure we don't infect anyone else?"

"Yes, Ma'am," Clint said, "I'm afraid that's what we'll have to do."

"And what if we don't want to go?" she asked. "What if we are tired of being pushed around by strangers?"

"I'm sorry, Ma'am," Clint said, "but I'm afraid I wouldn't be able to give you a choice."

"You'd force us?"

"Yes, Ma'am."

She remained silent for a moment, then said, "Well, I've seen what you're capable of."

"Ma'am?"

"You shot that man in cold blood."

"Yes, Ma'am," Clint said. "To put him out of his misery. He begged me to. You heard him."

"Yes, I did hear him," she said, "but I still don't believe that you had the right to kill him."

"Well," Clint said, "I guess we could debate that for a long time, Mrs. Grady."

"Tell me," she said, touching her face, "tell me again what the symptoms are?"

THIRTY-FOUR

When they ran into Cole, Grady and the boy on the way back, Mary Grady dismounted and ran toward them. Clint and Cole watched uncomfortably as the family of three was reunited. There were tears and many hugs and kisses while the two men looked away.

"What do we do now?" Cole asked.

"Let's ride back to where their wagon is and we'll camp there," Clint said. "In the morning we'll hitch two horses to the wagon and take them all back to Safetown with us."

"Okay."

"What about Tyler, Jace?" Clint asked. "Did he come in contact with anyone else?"

"Not that I know of."

"Was he . . . sick?"

"You mean, did he have it? The boy says no."

"I'll check with the mother."

"Robak had it?"

"Bad," Clint said.

"What did you do?"

141

Clint just looked at him.

"Oh."

"I touched him," Clint said.

"Oh . : . Jesus. Are you gonna . . . ?

"I guess we'll just have to wait and see," Clint said, "but just to be on the safe side you better not touch anything that I touch."

"What about Mr. Grady?" Cole asked. "Did he touch Robak?"

"It doesn't really matter, does it?" Clint asked. They looked at the family, still embracing. "He's touching them."

Back at the wagon, Joshua Grady was saying how unbelievable this all was.

"I can't believe that we're back together," he said, "and that we still have our belongings."

"And we have our team," Matthew said, "now that Mr. Adams said we can keep that man's horse."

He was talking about Tyler's horse. Clint had unsaddled Robak's horse and set it free. He'd buried Robak in a shallow grave and did the same for his belongings so no one else would come in contact with them. He wondered about the horse, but maybe if they weren't affected, the animals couldn't infect anyone else.

"Yes, we are back together," Mary Grady said, "but we have to go with Mr. Adams and Deputy Cole."

"But my job—"

"Joshua," she said, "if we go on to Sweethaven we might infect the entire town."

"Yes," he said, "of course, you're right."

Mary was doing the cooking, and Cole was so hungry he decided to just go ahead and eat.

"I'm travelling with you all," he said, "I might as well eat with you."

"You're a brave man," Mary Grady said.

"No, Ma'am," he said, accepting a plate of food from her, "I'm just a hungry one."

"You shoulda seen the deputy, Momma," Matthew said, excitedly. "He shot that man right out of his saddle."

"Don't say 'shoulda,' Matthew," his father scolded him.

"I'm sorry, Poppa," Matthew said.

"He's all excited, Joshua," Mary said. "Let him be for now."

"All right," Joshua said, reaching out to take her hand. "I can't deny you anything now that I have you back."

Clint and Cole ate away from the others. They still felt like they were eavesdropping on them, they seemed to be such a close family.

"We'll take the watch tonight, you and me," Clint said. "I'll go first, then you."

"Watching for what?" Cole asked. "Robak and Tyler are dead."

"We don't want anyone sneaking up on us and riding into camp," Clint said. "We've got to keep ourselves away from people, Jace."

"Oh, I see what you mean," the deputy said. "All right, Clint. I'll take the second watch."

While Clint was on watch, he heard someone behind him. When he turned he saw Mary Grady approaching him, her long hair tousled from the trials she'd gone through, and from having been lying on it while she slept—or tried to sleep. Even so, she was a beautiful woman.

"Can't sleep?" he asked.

"No," she said. "May I talk to you?"

"Sure. Coffee?"

"No, thank you."

She got down onto her knees across the fire from him.

"Mr. Adams, I feel I was rather harsh and unfair with you earlier today," she said. "I wish to apologize."

"No apology necessary, Mrs. Grady."

"Nevertheless, I'm giving it."

"Then I accept."

"And I wish you would call me Mary."

"All right, Mary. My name is Clint."

"Yes," Mary said. "I, uh, understand you are a man with a reputation."

"I'm afraid so."

"I want you to know I did not know that when I . . . judged you harshly today. It had nothing to do with what I said."

"All right."

"I mean . . . I was judging you by your actions, which at the time I thought . . . extreme."

"But not now?"

"No," she said. "I've given it some thought, and that poor man would have suffered. As awful as he was, it would not have been right to let him suffer like that."

"Well, Mary," Clint said, "I thank you for coming over to tell me that, but I think you better get some sleep now. We have a long trip ahead of us tomorrow, and I want to make it before nightfall."

"All right," she said, getting to her feet. "Thank you for accepting my apology."

"Thank you for offering it."

She stared at him a few moments longer, long enough to make him feel a little uncomfortable, and then she said, "Well, see you in the morning."

"See you then."

He turned and watched her walk back to her wagon and climb in, then poured himself another cup of coffee.

THIRTY-FIVE

"Whoa," Clint said, and he wasn't talking to his horse.

"What is it?" Cole asked.

Joshua Grady stopped his wagon right behind them and shouted, "What's wrong? Are we there?"

Cole turned and said, "It's just over that rise," pointing ahead of them.

"Then why are we stopping?"

Cole looked at Clint.

"Why *are* we stopping?"

"Because," Clint said, "the Gradys and I can't go into Safetown."

"Why not?"

"Because we have all definitely been in contact with an infected person," Clint said. "You have not."

"So what are you saying?"

"I'm saying you have to go to Safetown, while we have to go into Thanesville."

"No," Cole said, "that's crazy."

"No, it's not," Clint said. "Listen, you ride into Safe-

147

town and explain the situation to Jenny, then come back and tell me what she says."

Cole frowned.

"We're not going to go anywhere," Clint said. "We'll wait right here, and I'll explain the wait to the Gradys while you're gone."

"You won't move from here?" Cole asked.

"Not an inch."

"All right," Cole said. "I'll go and talk to Jenny, but I'll be right back, Clint."

"We'll be here," Clint said. "I'm just trying to stay on the safe side, Jace. That's all."

Cole nodded, then turned his horse and rode toward Safetown. Clint dismounted and walked back to tell the Grady family what was happening.

When Jace Cole came riding back, he seemed excited— or agitated. He was riding to them hell-for-leather, and Clint wondered if something had gone wrong in Safetown.

Finally, Jace Cole reached them and dismounted even before his horse came to a stop.

"It's over!"

"What?" Clint asked.

Cole stopped in front of Clint, completely out of breath.

"It's all over," he panted. "Jenny says Doc found a cure."

"A cure? Is he sure?"

"I don't know," Cole said. "All I know is what Jenny told me. She said you all can come into camp with no fear."

Clint wasn't sure about this. He wondered if he should

make the Grady family wait until he had spoken with Jenny, or with Doc Beacham, or maybe even Sheriff Ives.

"Clint," Cole said, "come on, it's over. We can all go back home."

"Have they pulled up stakes in Safetown?" Clint asked.

"Well, no," Cole said, "Jenny says there's still some work to be done. She'll tell you about it when you come in."

Well, Clint thought, Doc Beacham was never really all that sure that Safetown *was* actually safe.

"What's going on?" Joshua Grady asked. "Did I hear the deputy say there's a cure?"

"That's what he was told," Clint said. "All right, then, I guess we're going in to Safetown."

Joshua went back to his wagon, and Cole got back on his horse.

"This is the best news we coulda come back to," Cole said to Clint. "Isn't it?"

"It's good news, all right," Clint agreed. "If it's true."

THIRTY-SIX

As Clint, Jace Cole and the Grady family entered Safe-town Jenny came out to meet them, as well as Mayor Horace Russell. Both had big, beaming smiles on their faces.

"Did Jace tell you?" Jenny asked.

"It's a miracle," Russell said.

"It sounds like it," Clint said, dismounting. "How did it happen?"

"It was what you said about the animals, Clint," Jenny said. "Doc was able to make a serum out of something that was in the horses that made them immune."

"Has he tested the serum?"

"He's injected several infected people," she said, "and so far they've responded well. The progress of the disease has been arrested."

"But has the effect been reversed yet?"

"We're waiting to see for sure," Jenny said, "but Doc says it looks really good."

"Wait a minute," Clint said. "This is not a full-fledged cure yet? Jace said it was."

151

"I told him it probably was, and that you should come on in."

"Jenny," Clint said, "this is the Grady family. They were in contact with Ted Robak, who died of the disease."

"Oh," Jenny said. "And the others?"

"They're all dead," Clint said, "but not from the disease." And technically speaking, Robak had not died of the disease, either, but Clint did not bother to mention that.

"Well," Jenny said, "we'll have to get them into Thanesville, to Doc—"

"Let's get them someplace where they can rest, for now," Clint said.

"Of course," Jenny said. "I'll see to it."

She went past Clint to attend to the Grady family, and Horace Russell stepped up.

"Did I hear you say that Robak and his men were dead?"

"That's right."

"All of them?"

"Right again."

"And they didn't, uh, come in contact with anyone?"

"Only with this family," Clint said. "They took the mother and son hostage to try to hold us off."

"So you killed all six?"

"Jace and I did," Clint said.

"Cole was a help to you?"

"He was more than that," Clint said. "In fact, I was out there helping him."

"I'm sure Sheriff Ives will be glad to hear that his deputy did so well," Russell said.

"Look," Clint said, "when are you moving back into town?"

"As soon as we get the all-clear from Doc," Russell said. "We're getting packed up now."

As Clint looked around he could see that there was a lot of activity in the camp, and a lot more energy and smiles than when he left.

"I hope this is going to turn out all right," he said.

"Doc says he's got it beat," Russell said. "I believe him."

"I need a drink and some food, and so do these people," Clint said. "Maybe after that I can talk with Doc, and maybe finally get to see my friend Henry Ives."

"Go ahead and ride into town," Russell said. "I'm sure the sheriff will be happy to see you."

Clint watched as the Mayor also walked up to Joshua Grady and his family to greet them. They would all be glad when this was finally over, but he hoped that no one was throwing caution to the wind.

Clint looked up from his coffee and beans as Jenny Thane approached him.

"Can I join you?" she asked.

She crouched down by the fire and said, "I'll just have some coffee. I've had enough beans to last me a lifetime. It'll be nice to eat some normal food again once we get back to town."

"Have you been back to town yet, Jenny?"

"No, not yet," she said, 'but I'll be one of the first ones to go back. Why?"

"I want to go in and talk to Doc and to Henry Ives."

"Why? Are you worried about this cure?"

"When I left it was all doom and gloom around here,

and now everybody's happy and acting like it's all over, when in fact it isn't, is it?"

"Well," she said, "not quite."

"Jenny," he said, "I want this to be a cure as much as anybody, but let's not get cocky and put people in danger until we know for sure."

"Doc *is* making sure, Clint," she said. "He is."

"All the same," he said, "maybe you and I should ride into town later and have a talk with him. Is that all right with you?"

"That's fine with me," she said. After a moment she added, "I'm really glad you're back safely."

He smiled and said, "So am I."

THIRTY-SEVEN

"Why does Adams want to go to town?" Russell asked Jenny.

"He just wants to make sure that no mistakes are being made."

"He's going to tell Doc that he's making a mistake? Where does he get the gall—"

"I think he's done all of us a service, Uncle Horace," Jenny said. "If he wants to go into town to talk to Doc, I don't think we should try to stop him. Besides, he wants to see his friend, the sheriff."

"You stick close to him, Jenny," Russell said. "I want to know what he says to Doc and Ives—"

"All right—"

"—and what they say to him."

"What do you mean?"

"Never mind, dear," Horace Russell said to her. "Just be aware of where your loyalties lie."

Clint made sure that Joshua, Mary and Matthew Grady were settled in and being fed before he headed into town. He also stopped to see Deputy Jace Cole.

"You did a hell of a job out there, Jace," he said. "I just wanted to let you know."

"Thanks, Clint," Cole said. "I learned a heckuva lot from you in just a few days."

"You'll be a fine lawman if you pursue this as a career. I'm going to tell Sheriff Ives that when I see him."

"And when is that gonna be?"

"Just a little while," Clint said. "I'm going into town with Jenny."

"I wonder when we'll all be going back, Clint?"

"As soon as Doc gives the okay," Clint said. "Shouldn't be too long now."

"It will be nice to get things back to normal."

"What's normal, Jace?"

"What?"

"What's it like in Thanesville on a normal day?"

"Well," Cole said, "just like everywhere else, I guess. Everybody goes about their business. Why do you ask?"

"I'm just curious," Clint said. "I mean, I've never been to Thanesville. I wouldn't know what was normal and what wasn't."

"Well, I suppose it'll take a while to really get back to normal."

"And the town council will have to appoint a new member."

"Huh?"

"I mean, since Matt Foley . . . died, won't they need to name someone to take his place?"

"I don't think so."

"Why not?"

"Well, the town council has just always been the same people."

"They don't let anyone else in?"

"They haven't in all the years I've been here."

"And how long has that been?"

"All my life."

"And has Horace Russell been the mayor all that time?"

"As far back as I can remember."

"What about Jenny's father? Was he on the council when he was alive?"

"No."

"He wasn't?"

"Well, there was no town council until he died," Cole said.

"That sounds odd."

"He was in charge while he was alive," Cole said. "I guess maybe they couldn't really decide who would take his place, so they started the town council. I really don't understand it, myself. It's politics, I guess."

"I suppose," Clint said, thinking that the whole thing sounded odd to him. "So there's never been an election for mayor?"

"Nope."

"There you are," Jenny said, coming up behind Clint. "Are you ready to go?"

"I'm ready," Clint said. "See you later, Jace."

He and Jenny walked over to their horses. They mounted up and started riding toward town.

"What were you and Jace talking about?" she asked.

"Politics."

"What's he know about politics?" she asked, with a laugh.

"Well, he told me that your uncle Horace has been mayor as far back as he can remember, and that there's never been an election," Clint said. "Is he right?"

She frowned and said, "I suppose he is."

"You don't know if there's been an election?"

"Well, maybe the council votes him in as mayor every year."

"And the townspeople don't get to vote?"

"I guess not," she said. "Why, is it done different in other towns?"

"It's done a whole lot different in other towns, Jenny," he said, and he wondered what else about Thanesville was different from other towns, as well.

THIRTY-EIGHT

When Clint got his first look at the town of Thanesville, it looked a lot like other towns. Maybe it was just the inner workings of the town that were different from others.

He did not question Jenny anymore about the town as they rode in. He decided to save that for a conversation with Henry Ives. But first he wanted to talk to Doc Beacham about this cure. He didn't claim to have any medical knowledge, but it did seem awfully soon to him for anyone to declare an epidemic to be over.

"Doc's office is over here," Jenny said, and then pointed and said, "Henry Ives is over there."

Clint looked across the street at the sheriff's office. It was a stone building with a heavy wooden door and two windows, one on either side.

"Let's talk to Doc first," he said.

They reined in in front of the doctor's office and dismounted. Jenny led the way and they entered without knocking first.

"Doc?" she called, when they saw that the room they

were in was empty. "Maybe he's in his surgery."

She walked to another door, opened it and looked in. "Not there."

"Maybe he's out treating patients," Clint said.

"Do you want to try to find him?" she asked.

"No," Clint said. "Let's go see if Ives is in his office."

"All right."

Once again Jenny led the way. They left the doctor's office and crossed over to the sheriff's. They entered without knocking and found the office to be as empty as the doc's.

"Maybe he's making his rounds."

Suddenly, Jenny smiled at Clint and said, "I think I might have an idea where Henry is."

Oh?" he asked. "Where?"

Henry Ives rolled over in bed and propped himself up on one elbow.

"What's wrong?" Hannah asked.

"Nothing."

"Come on, Henry," she said. "I know when something's bothering you. What is it?"

"It's Doc," Ives said.

"What about him?"

"He's so all-fired sure he's got a cure he's ready to let everyone from Safetown come back into town."

"And you're not?"

"Not what?" he asked. "Not sure about a cure? How do I know? I'm not a doctor. Not sure about letting everyone come back? Yeah, that's right. I'm not so sure it's a good idea—yet."

"So then, tell him."

"He's so excited about his discovery he's not even listening to me when I talk."

"Well, you should be happy about one thing," she said.

"Would that be you?" he asked.

"Well, that too," she answered, "but I meant your friend Clint Adams. He'll be coming into town with all the rest."

"You're right," Ives said, "he will." Suddenly, he sat up.

"What is it?"

"I'd better get dressed."

"Why?"

"Because we don't know when he'll be coming in," he said, "and he'll look for me in my office."

"Is this just an excuse to get away from me?"

He looked down at her, at her big breasts with large, dark nipples and pale skin, and said, "Why would I ever want to get away from you?"

"Where?" Clint asked.

"He's got a woman," Jenny said.

"Henry has?"

"Yes," Jenny said. "They've know each other a long time, but they never did anything until this epidemic brought them close together."

"Well," Clint said, "good for Henry."

They were out in front of the sheriff's office now, trying to decide their next move.

"He's probably with her."

"And where does she live?"

"She has a room at the hotel."

"The hotel?" Clint asked. "Isn't she from here?"

"Yes. Several people have permanent rooms at the hotel. Do you want to go over there and see if he's there?"

"I don't know that I want to bother him," Clint said, "or walk in on anything—"

"Wait," she said.

"For what?"

"There he is," she said, "coming out of the hotel now."

Clint looked across the street and, sure enough, saw his friend Sheriff Henry Ives coming out of the hotel.

THIRTY-NINE

"Hello, Henry," Clint greeted as the man reached them.

"Hello, Clint," the sheriff said. He extended his hand and Clint took it. "Good to see you. It's been a long time."

"A very long time, Henry," Clint said. "You've changed."

"Lost weight."

"A lot of weight."

Ives touched his hat and said, "And maybe some hair."

"We're all losing hair," Clint said.

"Hello, Sheriff," Jenny said.

"Hi, Jenny," Ives said. "It's really nice to see you again."

"Sheriff, do you know where Doc is?" she asked.

"He's not in his office?"

"No."

"He must be making his rounds, then," Ives said. "Checking on the people he injected with his serum."

"Would you know who those people are?" Clint asked.

"I'm afraid not," Ives said. "Do you two want to come inside? I'll make some coffee."

"Not right now, Henry," Clint said, cutting Jenny off. "I'd like to find the doctor."

"Oh? Why's that?"

"I want to talk to him about this cure of his."

"Nothing short of a miracle for this town," Ives said.

"I guess so," Clint said. "Still, I'd just like to talk to him, for my own piece of mind. After all, I can't leave here unless he gives it to me, too, right?"

"I guess that's right."

"Jenny tells me you met a woman."

Ives smiled.

"Met her a while ago," he said, "but somehow this . . . experience has brought us closer together."

"I think it's wonderfully romantic," Jenny said.

Ives looked at Clint and said, "Women."

"They think everything is romantic."

"Well," Ives said, "when you want to talk to me, Clint, I'll be in my office. I'll have the coffee ready."

"Okay, Henry," Clint said. "I'll see you later."

"Yeah," Ives said, "later."

He opened the door to his office and went inside. When he had closed the door again he leaned back against it, took off his hat and wiped the sweat from his brow—sweat that had nothing to do with any kind of disease.

"I thought you wanted to talk to Henry," Jenny asked.

"Not now," Clint said. "Is there someplace you and I could go to talk?"

"Well," she said, "I don't know what's open—"

"How about where you live?"

She shook her head.

"It's been so long since I was there I forgot," she said. "I have a couple of rooms two blocks from here."

"Let's go there."

"Well, all right," she said, "but can you tell me—"

"I'll explain when we're alone and off the street," Clint said. "Lead the way, Jenny."

When they entered her rooms they had a musty smell to them.

"I'll open a window to air it out," she said, but he grabbed her arm and stopped her.

"Never mind that," he said, "we have to talk."

"First you wanted to talk to Doc, then to Henry, and now to me?" she asked. "You had your chance to talk to Henry, why didn't you take it?"

"I would have," he said, "except for one thing."

"What's that?"

"That man was not Henry Ives."

FORTY

"Not the Henry Ives I knew, anyway."

"Now wait," Jenny said. "I heard you both say it's been a long time since you've seen each other."

"About twelve years."

"A lot can happen to a man in twelve years," she said.

"Okay, look," Clint said, "he's close, very close. He looks like him and sounds like him. Somebody's obviously gone to a lot of trouble to find this man to replace him, but that is not Henry Ives."

"Okay," Jenny said, "he's been Henry Ives since I've known him."

"And how long has that been?"

"Since I came back to town from the east," she said.

"Then he was brought to replace the real Ives before that."

"Wait," Jenny said, "are you sure your 'real' Henry Ives was ever really sheriff here?"

"I'm sure."

"How?"

"Other friends saw him here."

"How long ago?"

"Years."

"I don't understand," she said. "Why would anyone go to the trouble of finding a . . . a double for your friend?"

"Maybe because they killed him?"

"Who killed him?"

"Who hired him?"

"He was hired by Uncle Horace and the rest of the board."

"And what about this board?" he asked. "How come nobody else is allowed on it?"

"When it was formed, following my father's death, they all agreed that they would be the only members. If one of them left, or died, he would not be replaced."

"And was it agreed that Horace Russell would always be mayor?"

"I told you," she said, "they voted him in, and I guess they keep him in."

"Come on, Jenny," he said. "That doesn't sound odd to you? When you were back east didn't you see some elections?"

"I never paid attention to politics."

"Okay," Clint said, "let's forget politics. Let's talk about murder."

"Murder?"

He nodded.

"Someone murdered Henry Ives and replaced him with this man," Clint said.

"You think it was someone on the board?"

"It had to be," he said, "or maybe it's the whole board."

"Uncle Horace and Doc would never kill anyone.

What about this epidemic, Clint? Do you think this was fake?"

"It wasn't fake," Clint said, "because I saw the bodies, but I think it was unfortunate."

"That's what you'd call it? Unfortunate? How can you say that?"

"Unfortunate for the fake Henry Ives and the men who hired him," Clint said. "It threatened to bring attention to the town, outside attention. I was wondering why Doc hadn't called for outside help. Weren't you?"

"Well . . ."

"They must have panicked when it broke out and panicked even more when my telegram arrived."

"Why didn't he leave, then?"

"Because then I'd wonder where the real Ives was," Clint said. "So they decided to try to fool me with this one."

"But . . . what about Hannah?"

"She's obviously in love with this Ives," he said. "I have no idea how she felt about the real one. Maybe she can't tell the difference."

"She can't tell the difference between the man she loved and a phony?" Jenny asked.

"You said yourself they went slow, that it was only this epidemic that brought them together. So she's never slept with anyone but this Ives."

"This all sounds crazy," she said. "You're accusing the town fathers here of murdering their own lawman, and then replacing him with a look-alike?"

"You know what?" Clint asked. "That's exactly what I'm accusing them of."

•   •   •

Since Clint did trust the "sheriff," they decided to go and find Doc Beacham. They checked his office again and this time they found him in.

"Mr. Adams!" Doc said, as they entered. "My boy, you are a genius. I don't know why I didn't take notice myself of the fact that the animals had not been affected. It was sheer inspiration."

"You were just too close to the problem, Doctor," Clint said. "But Doc, are you sure this is a cure?"

"As of this morning, positive," the older man said. "I have checked all of the patients I injected yesterday, and their symptoms are gone. We've cured it, my boy!"

"You cured it, Doc," Clint said. "Congratulations."

"Jenny," Doc said, "the people out in Safetown can start returning anytime. I'll have to give everyone in town a shot, though."

"Uh, maybe we better hold off on everybody coming back to town for a while, Doc," Clint said.

"Whatever for?" Doc asked. "The epidemic is over, my boy. They can all come home."

"Clint has a different problem he wants to ask you about, Doc."

"Oh?" Doc looked at Clint. "And what's that?"

"Doc," Clint said, "I need to know who killed the real Henry Ives."

FORTY-ONE

Doc Beacham stared at Clint for a few moments, and just when Clint was sure he was going to lie, his shoulders slumped and he sat down heavily.

"Doc?" Jenny said.

"I'm just too tired to lie, Jenny, dear," he said.

"You mean . . . the sheriff isn't the real Henry Ives?"

"He is now," Doc said, "but he wasn't always."

"You'll have to explain that one to me, Doc," Clint said. "You see, the real Ives was my friend twelve years ago. This man looks like him, and sounds like him, but that's about it."

"It's really very simple," Doc said. "Henry Ives was hired to be our sheriff. As it turned out, he wasn't a very good one."

"I don't think that's—"

"Oh, don't get me wrong," the doctor said. "He was fair enough, and a good enough lawman, but just not suited to this town and the way things were done here."

Clint stared at the man.

"You see, after Jenny's father died, Horace and I and

some of the others, we formed the town council. We decided Horace would be mayor, and we called ourselves the Seven."

"And you ran this town."

"Yes."

"No elections, right?"

"No, none," Doc said, "and the town didn't mind, really. I mean, Jenny's father was my friend, but he ruled with an iron hand, and the town chafed beneath it. When we took over . . . well, everybody sort of preferred it."

"Except Henry Ives?"

Doc closed his eyes and nodded.

"We voted on hiring him and he got the job, four votes to three. Horace voted against. So did Matt Foley and Sam Evers. The rest of us voted him in." Doc shook his head. "It was a big mistake."

"You said he was a good lawman."

"He didn't like the way things were run," Doc said. "He threatened all kinds of things if there weren't some changes."

"And you seven didn't want to change?"

"No."

"So you killed him."

Doc looked directly into Clint's eyes now and held them steadily.

"You have to believe me, now, when I say I don't know who killed Henry Ives all those years ago."

"How many, Doc?"

"Oh . . . ten, maybe nine. I can't remember."

"So what happened? Did he just disappear?"

"Oh, no," Doc said, "he was killed, right in his office. He was found behind his desk, shot."

"Found by who?"

"One of the Seven."

"No one heard the shot?"

"If they did, they never said."

"So instead of trying to find out who did it," Clint said, "the Seven decided to hire a look-alike?"

"It was either that or suffer outside interference," Doc said. "They were—we've always been afraid that some-one would come in from outside and make us change."

"Where did the look-alike come from?" Clint asked.

"That you'll have to ask Horace," Doc said. "He and Sam left town and came back with this Henry Ives. He was installed in the sheriff's office as if nothing had happened."

"And?"

"And he became Henry Ives," Doc said. "I don't know what his name was before, but he's been Henry Ives all these years."

"Well," Clint said, "not anymore."

"What are you going to do?" Doc asked.

"I can't just let this go, Doc," Clint said. "My friend was killed."

"What kind of friend were you that you haven't seen him in twelve years?" Doc asked.

"I'm a busy man who travels a lot and has a lot of friends, Doc," Clint said. "I may not see them all that often, but I value every one of them."

"So, you're going to expose us?"

"I have no choice."

"Horace isn't going to like that."

"That's too bad."

"Jenny, girl?" Doc said.

"Yes, Doc?"

"Would you go outside, please, and wait?"

"Why, Doc?"

"Please," he said. "Humor an old man. Wait outside while I talk to Mr. Adams."

"Doc—"

"Go ahead, Jenny," Clint said. "I want to hear what Doc has to say, and he doesn't want you to hear it."

She stared at the two men for a moment, then turned and walked out of the room.

"All right, Doc," Clint said. "What's on your mind?"

FORTY-TWO

"I'll tell you exactly what's on my mind, Mr. Adams," Doc Beacham said. "Your health."

"Are you threatening me, Doc?"

"I'm telling you," Doc said, "that without my serum you may fall prey to this disease and die a very ugly death."

"So you'd withhold the serum from me unless I keep my mouth closed? To cover for your friends?"

"For my town," Doc said.

"Doc," Clint said, "we live in a democracy—at least, I do. I don't know what you live in, but I'll tell you where you don't live—in a town where you can arbitrarily kill a lawman who gets in your way."

"The serum—"

"What makes you think that I won't agree just to get the serum, and then do what I want afterward?"

"I'll accept your word."

"I may not get the disease," Clint reminded him, "or need your serum, Doc, so I don't think I can give it to you."

"Are you willing to take that chance?"

"If it's either that or forget that my friend was killed," Clint said, "I guess I'll have to take my chances."

"No," Jenny said, sticking her head in the door, "you won't."

"Jenny!" Doc said.

She came into the room and said, "You asked me to leave the room, you didn't say I couldn't listen at the door. I'm ashamed of you, Doc."

"My dear—"

"If you don't give Clint the serum, I will." She looked at Clint. "You needn't worry about making that decision, Clint."

"My dear," Doc said, "if Horace was here he'd remind you of your loyalty."

"He already did that, Doc," Jenny said, "and I've always been loyal to the town, and to you and Uncle Horace, Doc—but that was when I didn't know you'd killed someone."

"I didn't kill anyone—"

"You covered it up," Clint said. "That makes you just as guilty as whoever pulled the trigger."

"Clint," Jenny said, "you do what you've got to do. I'll back you up, and make sure you get the serum."

"Doc," Clint said, "you've done a wonderful thing, coming up with that serum—"

"Thank you—"

"—but if you'd sent for help when this all started, someone else might have thought about the animals long before I did, and a lot of people might not have died. You talk about loyalty, but what about your oath? What about your loyalty to that? You put loyalty to a town, and to men who were guilty of murder, above that."

Doc shook his head and said, "I'm an old man—"

"But you weren't always an old man," Clint said, cutting him off, "so that's no excuse."

Clint walked to the door.

"I'm leaving now," he said. "One of your own board died of this disease, so I guess that makes you the Six now. You better talk to your other council members and tell them what's going on."

"They—they might try to kill you."

"I doubt it," Clint said. "I won't be sitting in an office, and they won't be able to approach me under the guise of friendship. They would have to come right at me, and which of them is going to do that?"

"Perhaps the sheriff," Doc said.

"A man who isn't really the sheriff, after all," Clint said, "no matter how long he's worn that badge."

"Where are you going?" Doc asked.

Clint turned and looked at him and said, "I'm going to take that badge away from him."

FORTY-THREE

The fake Henry Ives looked up from his desk as Clint entered the sheriff's office. He'd congratulated himself earlier on passing the ultimate test, but now he wasn't so sure.

"Clint, back so soon?"

"Let me ask you something?"

"Go ahead."

"How did you expect to get away with this?"

"I . . . don't know what you mean."

"Sure, you do," Clint said. "What if I started to reminisce about old times? How would you respond to that? Would you say, 'Well, it's been a long time,' and expect me to buy that?"

The man sat back in his chair and stared at Clint. His gun was still on his hip, a fact that Clint was very aware of. Instead of going for it, though, "Ives" folded his hands on his lap.

"I suppose," he said, "I was hoping this would be a quick visit and I wouldn't have to deal with that."

"Well, sorry to disappoint you," Clint said. "What did

they tell you, years ago, about this job? Did they say why they needed you to replace their sheriff?"

"Not in so many words, but I got the idea."

"So you've been living a lie all these years."

"No," the man said, "not a lie. I became Henry Ives. Everyone here accepted me as Henry Ives. I—I don't even know if I remember my own real name. Actually, yes I do. It's Henry Ives."

"No," Clint said, "that's a name you stole, and a life you stole, and I won't stand for it."

"What's it to you, Adams?" the man asked. "Why do you care what happens in this town?"

"I wouldn't care," Clint said, "if my friend wasn't dead. If not for that I'd leave here and be happy to leave you all to your little undemocratic society. But he is dead, and I can't just walk away."

"You're takin' away my life, here," the man said. "I've got a home, a woman—"

"A woman who doesn't even know your real name. It's not your life I'm taking away, friend. You'll just have to try to remember who you were before all this happened and go back to being that person. That is, if you leave this town alive."

The phony Ives stared at Clint, his hands still in his lap, and then he unclasped them.

"Want to make a try?" Clint asked.

No answer.

"Go ahead, why don't you do it?" Clint said. "I'm just mad enough to kill you and not care."

He watched the man's hands as they wavered in the air for a few moments before he finally put them flat on the desk.

"Take off the badge," Clint said, his tone cold. "It doesn't belong to you. It never did."

Clint was one of the first ones that day to be given the serum that would officially end the epidemic.

He didn't care if the phony Ives' woman would understand when he told her the truth; whether or not Doc Beacham reported the epidemic to the proper authorities, along with his cure, was not his concern.

All Clint did was send for a federal marshal so he could tell him the story of Sheriff Henry Ives, how he'd lived and died and been replaced. All he cared about was that his friend was somehow avenged, all these years later. Let the federal marshal deal with the "Six" and their odd way of running a town.

A town which—right at that moment—did not have any law of its own.

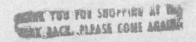

Watch for

THE SIOUX CITY WAR

228th novel in the exciting GUNSMITH series
from Jove

Coming in December!

J. R. ROBERTS
THE GUNSMITH